RETURN TO
BUTTERFLY ISLAND

After thirty years' absence, China Stuart returns to her birth place, the remote island of West Uist, to attend her aunt Beatrice's funeral — and finds she has inherited Stuart Grange. As if the funeral isn't traumatic enough, James McKriven, a land developer, is claiming the rights to China's ancestral home. Amongst the cobwebs and the cracked ceilings, China finds love, but faces the ghosts of the past . . . and the reason her family fled the island all those years ago.

RIKKI SHARP

RETURN TO BUTTERFLY ISLAND

LINFORD
Leicester

First published in Great Britain in 2010

First Linford Edition
published 2011

British Library CIP Data

Sharp, Rikki.
 Return to Butterfly Island. - -
 (Linford romance library)
 1. Inheritance and succession- -Fiction.
 2. Love stories. 3. Large type books.
 I. Title II. Series
 823.9′2–dc22

 ISBN 978–1–4448–0851–3

Published by
F. A. Thorpe (Publishing)
Anstey, Leicestershire

Set by Words & Graphics Ltd.
Anstey, Leicestershire
Printed and bound in Great Britain by
T. J. International Ltd., Padstow, Cornwall

This book is printed on acid-free paper

1

As the tiny fishing boat braved the wild sea swell, China Stuart wondered if she had made the right decision to venture into the middle of nowhere. Bundled up in borrowed jumpers and oilskins three sizes too large, her hair plastered in wet strands across her face, she clung to the ship's rail, refusing to shelter in the cabin, and trying not to be seasick.

It was that first view of the island she was waiting for. An image that had hidden in the edge of her dreams for as long as she could remember.

To most people it was just a lump of weathered rock sticking out of the ocean, just another dot on the map amongst the Outer Hebrides. But to China it was where she had been born. Having left with her mother when she was only six, after her father had been lost at sea, she had constantly dreamed of the wide-open

1

skies and the rugged rock-strewn fields. Finally, she would see if the truth matched her childhood fantasies.

After almost 30 years away she was coming home, but not for the best of reasons. China's last living relative had passed away in her sleep three days previously. Although her solicitor had explained that, as Aunt Bee had requested to be buried on the island, the ancient family house and various stretches of land around it could be disposed of comfortably from Manchester, China had been suddenly struck with a stubborn compulsion and she felt honour-bound to sort the Stuart estate out in person.

But as she fought to keep what was left of her lunch down, she was now having serious doubts about the whole adventure.

★ ★ ★

'You're going where?' Anthony had asked. He was her best friend in the world and a co-worker at Slater and

Marsh, a top-end advertising agency in Manchester city centre. She had pointed at the map she had just purchased especially for the occasion. Eleven miles by six in size, its true name was West Uist, but she remembered it by the name her father always used — Butterfly Island. Then he had been the romantic in the family.

'It doesn't even have any proper roads!' exclaimed Anthony.

'No need for them. No cars.'

'You have lost the plot; girlfriend,' he pouted.

She had laughed and ruffled his too-perfect hair. 'Imagine that stiff Atlantic breeze in your hair, and drying out that peach-like skin of yours . . . '

'Stop it! I won't sleep tonight. But you are coming back, aren't you? Who else will put up with my hissy fits in this place?'

'Of course I'm coming back. This is just something I need to do. Put a few old ghosts to rest.'

* * *

Ghosts to rest . . . wasn't that the truth? Even as a teenager China had felt there was a wall between herself and her mother because of the sudden way they had left the island. They had never talked about those years, as if that idyllic life on West Uist with her father had never happened. Then her mother had died suddenly of a heart problem ten years previously, leaving so much unsaid. What answers she would find amongst the windswept rocks and heather, she had absolutely no idea.

Finally she saw it; a line of blue and grey rock between the scudding clouds and the rolling ocean. Butterfly Island — indigenous population of exactly 75. If you didn't farm or fish yourself, then you took care of those who did. She smiled, the salty water dripping off the end of her freezing nose. Well here comes number 76. Cancel those previous self-doubts. This had been the right way to say goodbye to her Aunt and to exhume a family past muddled in mystery.

'I must be absolutely barking,' China whispered to herself, as she finally set foot on dry land after the hour-and-a-half sea journey. The crude stone jetty they were now moored to joined a cinder track that swept past a cluster of weather-worn cottages and several massive corrugated iron boat houses. The largest of these ancient cottages was a pub of sorts, with the odd name of The Cuckoo Inn.

'Let's get you into the Inn before this weather breaks, lass,' said John Dart, the Skipper of the fishing boat that had collected her from one of the major islands, Benbecula. Whereas North and South Uist were connected to Benbecula by raised stone causeways, West Uist could be only reached by sea, or on special occasions by helicopter, stuck as it was all by itself between the Inner and Outer Hebrides.

'Inn? I'll be staying at the Grange, won't I? Aunt Bea's place?'

'Ah, well . . . ' muttered the Skipper. 'Wait until you see the state of the place. Beatrice had rather let things slide of recent years.'

So, like it or not, China was towed in the Skipper's wake towards the stone-built whitewashed pub. As they passed three scruffy looking children, the bairns stared with wide-open eyes at the stranger, never saying a word. Then, as one, the tykes turned and ran through a sudden squall of rain, Wellington boots splashing China as they raced passed.

'Hey!' she shouted, as if she wasn't wet enough already.

'Never mind them,' the Skipper cried from The Cuckoo. 'Storm's up!'

And down came the rain.

Welcome home, China thought as she raced for the shelter of the inn, wondering just what she'd discover here about her past . . .

*   *   *

Like a drowned rat, China stumbled into the ancient tap room, her usually well groomed explosion of dark blonde curls sticking out at all angles from under a borrowed woollen hat. Sneezing three times, she stood on the checkered linoleum floor in an expanding puddle, suddenly realising everyone in the pub was looking at her. 'Hi,' was all she could get out.

It was a silent interrogation. Old whiskery men in heavy coats, younger fishermen in oilskins and sou'westers, and the comfortably built landlady from behind the bar all stared back at her.

Skipper John cleared his throat. 'This is China Stuart, Beatrice's niece from Manchester. Here to pay her last respects and see to the Grange.'

The silence was suddenly broken. Murmurs of understanding and even one or two good intentioned nods came from the islanders, as they returned to their ale and dominos. But the quiet conversations that resumed were noticeably in Gaelic. To the islanders it was their first language, but to China it seemed as if they were rudely shutting her out.

One man stood out from the rest;

probably a couple of years older than China. He had sandy hair with a week old beard, and he actually managed a smile. There were deep laughter lines around his soft grey eyes and he was tanned by many years working at sea. Something tugged at her childhood memories. Running through the course grass hand in hand with a young boy and a cloud of coloured wings rising up into the air before them.

'This is my boy, Donald,' said the Skipper. 'You might remember him from years ago.'

'She won't, Pa. But I remember her. Wee China Stuart, hiding behind her mammy's skirts!'

China felt herself redden. 'Pardon?' she asked. Donald Dart just laughed.

The Skipper scowled at his son. 'Back in the day, you two used to play with each other all the time, up at the Grange. Sometimes my brainless boy can put on the thick Gaelic accent for the tourists. A little respect, Donald, she's a Stuart, after all!'

'Was a Stuart, thirty years ago. She left, remember?' And with that unexpected outburst, Donald finished his beer and stamped out into the torrential rain.

'Not one of my family's biggest fans then, your son?' said China, trying to wrestle her hair into some sort of order.

'On the contrary. He was awful fond of Beatrice, even though she could be a bit tetchy in her later years. Donald used to do a few odd jobs for her, trying to keep that old pile o' stones from falling down.'

Thanking the Skipper for the ride to the island, China let the landlady, Mrs Baxter lead her up to a tiny bedroom on the second floor.

'Bathroom's down the hall, Miss Stuart. There's hot water in the tank now, and I've left sandwiches by the bed. Oh, and there was a pile of mail Donald brought down from the Grange; some of it was addressed to you.'

China thanked Mrs Baxter, dying to get out of the clinging wet clothes.

Exhausted, she closed the bedroom door and turned the key in the lock, feeling totally out of her comfort zone. All these strange people with their nearly incomprehensible accents, was this what she had wanted to return to? Still, she had come here with a dual purpose — see off her Aunt in proper Stuart style and to try to find her roots, so she had better get used to things pretty quickly. It was as she shrugged off the oilskins, that she suddenly realised she was not alone in the room. Someone was watching her.

Laying on the single bed was the scruffiest dog she had ever seen. An Irish wolfhound the size of a small pony, he was just finishing off a large plate of sandwiches. The dog looked at her as he licked the last of her meal from his whiskers. Blinking rapidly in surprise, China swore quite fluently, then waved one finger at the beast and scolded, 'Bad dog!' Improvising her belt as a lead, she dragged the bedraggled spiky-haired mutt down the twisted staircase and back into the pub.

'This, whatever-his-name-is was in my room,' she said to Mrs Baxter.

'Aye, that'll be right. This is Morgan. He belongs to you.'

China gasped for a few moments like a fish out of water. 'Me?' she eventually squeaked.

'He was Beatrice's dog. We've been looking after him since she passed, so now he's yours.'

Morgan panted and looked at her through tangled grey fur, then casually slipped his lead and padded back upstairs to the bedroom.

'Oh,' was all China could get out. The only pet she had had as a child was a goldfish, Blinky. He had lasted two weeks. Trying to retain a little dignity, she stuck her nose in the air and followed the dog back upstairs.

Morgan, although the friendliest animal in creation, did what dogs do best — smelt terrible. Using up most of the precious hot water, China gave him a long bath. Enjoying the unusual experience, Morgan soaked her through by way of thanks with a wild watery shake that began with his floppy ears and finally quivered out of the tip of his tail.

Recovering from that experience, after drying herself down, China spent five minutes looking through the letters Mrs Baxter had left in her room. Most were junk mail, but there was one in particular that looked very official, and when she read its contents it confused her greatly. Washing herself with what was left of the lukewarm water, hunger gnawed at her empty stomach.

'Bad dog,' she scowled at Morgan. He grinned at her in his doggie way and wagged his tail. Obviously used to being called that, she thought glumly. Putting on a warm Aran jumper and jeans, having a half-hearted attempt at brushing her curly hair into some sort of order, China tiptoed down the rickety stairs to find the pub almost completely in darkness.

'Hello?' she called out softly, seeing a

solitary figure hunched at the bar.

'Hello yourself,' replied a familiar voice. In the faint golden lights from above the bar, Donald Dart smiled at her, a glass of malt whisky warming in his hands. 'We're sort of closed. Sorry about earlier. You caught me by surprise. I never thought you'd come back just for the funeral.'

She joined him at the bar, slipping onto the worn barstool next to him. In the soft light he looked a little less windswept, but just as interesting. Trying not to salivate, she eyed up his supper — a large slice of game pie and a thick cheese sandwich on home baked bread.

'That's me, all impulsive and wild,' she laughed, hoping her jocular tone didn't sound too false. Why was she nervous around Donald? They had been kids when she had first known him. It annoyed her that she remembered so little about that time.

Donald nodded and slipped casually behind the bar. Topping up his own drink from the optic, he poured a second glass and slid it across the polished mahogany towards her.

'On the house. Biddy won't mind, she's my da's sister. We're nearly all related on the island. If you're hungry, help yourself. I've had my fill.'

Without being asked twice, China wolfed down the sandwich first then attacked the pie. As she ate, the great lopping form of Morgan suddenly appeared at her side, tongue lolling out, looking wistfully at the chunk of pie in her hands.

'He's sticking to you like glue,' Donald chuckled. When he smiled, all that anger seemed to wash away, his grey eyes full of energy and memories. China suddenly felt comfortable in his presence. Safe. Unthreatened.

'He's just after the food. He already polished off my supper.'

'That's what Morgan does best. Food up at the Grange was a wee bit scarce most days, so he's turned into a bit of a scrounger.'

China wrinkled her nose. 'A smelly one at that.' She fumbled in her jeans pocket for a creased envelope. 'This was waiting for me, along with the Hound of the Baskervilles here. What do you make of it?'

As he reached to take the letter, their fingers brushed against each other. China suddenly found herself becoming slightly flushed and was glad of the low lighting. She put it down to the strong whisky, but it didn't stop her from staring at Donald. This just so wasn't like her.

Reading the contents of the letter quickly, a touch of the old angry Donald surfaced for an instant, as he screwed the A4 sheet of paper into a ball and lobbed it into the darkness of the pub snug.

'Damn parasite! This keeps happening all across the local islands when anyone elderly is ill or dies.'

China glanced at the expensive looking stamp on the envelope. 'James McKriven, Na h-Eileanan Siar Property

Developers. Sounds posh.'

'It means, 'Western Isles' in Gaelic. Not that McKriven speaks the tongue. Him and his bloody family have been plundering the islands as long as there have been people on them.'

By this time, Morgan had retrieved the scrunched up letter and dropped it, only slightly damp, into China's hand. Flattening it out on the bar top she read it again, a worried frown creasing her brow.

'But it says here my Aunt has given first option to this company. That their claim to the Grange and the surrounding acreage supersedes mine.'

'We'll have to see about that. I'm sure McKriven is just chancing his arm. You'll need Bea's solicitor, Douglas McGregor to look into it tomorrow. You look all done in.'

She was. The excitement and the stress of the long journey to Butterfly Island had finally taken its toll and China found she was warm, comfortable and couldn't keep her eyes open.

Helping her up the first few stairs to her tiny room, with Morgan leading the way, Donald reluctantly let her go.

'See you in the morning . . . ' he whispered. Then she turned on the stair, leaning down, and kissed him softly on the cheek. It was the fisherman's turn to blush.

'Thanks for the pie,' she said as she vanished up the twisting staircase.

'Thanks for coming back,' he replied. But she had already shut the door to her room behind her.

Enclosed in a small space with the massive dog once again, the bath seemed to have made his natural odour worse. As the weather was still too wild outside to open a window, China spent the night with her head under the bed covers to avoid the smell of damp dog. Morgan curled up on one of her suitcases and began to snore softly.

China slept fitfully to start with, plagued by ancient dreams. In her sleep, half recalled memories started to come back to her down the forgotten years, not all of them pleasant ones. But there was always the tousled haired Donald there, holding her hand, looking after her.

Pulling the massive quilt tighter, China Stuart settled into a deeper sleep with a smile on her face as the wind howled around The Cuckoo like something possessed. Yet she found the storm strangely soothing. In her dreams, she wondered what the new day would bring.

2

The following morning was the day before the funeral. By some divine miracle the rain had finally stopped, the clouds dispersed and the sky turned an ice blue. Morgan woke China up with loving licks around her face, despite her protests. Squinting at her watch she was horrified to find it was only half past five in the morning.

Guilt stopped her from turning over and trying to get back to sleep, as she suddenly remembered she had promised to ring Anthony back in Manchester the minute she set foot on that tiny dot in the Minch — the Sea of the Hebrides. Of course, even when she waved her mobile around standing on her bed, she couldn't get a signal. She was sure she had seen a mast just behind the pub, but maybe The Cuckoo was in a dead zone.

'Sorry Anthony,' she said to herself as she washed and dressed, staring up at the piercing blue sky through the room's skylight. This was the island China remembered from her childhood. Long walks to the tiny stone Kirk, the wind ruffling the course grass into waves that rippled down from the hillside. The air so fresh that if you could have bottled it you'd have made a fortune, and the smell of the sea all around her.

Breakfast, consisting of toast, sausages, bacon and egg with a steaming pot of coffee, was waiting for her on the bar as the homely Mrs Baxter was up and about polishing the antique round tables.

'I'm starving!' China cried, tucking into the pile of fresh toast. 'How did you know I was up?'

'The water pipes in this old place tell a story every morning, banging and whistling. And that'll be the sea air giving you an appetite. You could do with a few square meals inside of you

— there's nothing of you, lassie!'

The hours spent in her expensive gym back in Manchester to keep that trim figure suddenly faced off against the pile of carbs before her. The bread won, and she slipped Morgan a sausage as he leaned against her legs, appearing by magic at the smell of cooking as usual. He certainly seemed to have taken a shine to her, and she hoped it wasn't all for food.

'That hairy con-artist has already had his breakfast!' Mrs Baxter scowled at the dog. Morgan's ears went down and he tried to hide under China's stool. 'And Donald's waiting outside,' the landlady let slip as she dusted the various paintings adorning the snug. There was a mischievous twinkle in her eyes as she told China this. 'He says he'll take you up to the Grange.'

Although China thought she remembered the way, the idea of spending a couple of hours in the fisherman's company rather pleased her. Demolishing the remainder of her breakfast, she grabbed her coat from upstairs and raced Morgan for the front door. The fresh air hit her like a solid wall. She closed her eyes and just soaked it all in.

Donald rose from the wooden bench at the front of the pub dressed in the same oilskins she'd first seen him in. But he looked as if he had attempted a shave and had put a comb through his untidy hair. China felt honoured. As he fussed the massive dog, he pointed back up the natural slope of the island, towards the woodland over its hills.

'Remember the way?'

'Try and catch me!' She laughed and ran on ahead, her boots splashing through the puddles left from the previous night's storm.

He let her win for a few hundred yards, of course. It was all part of the game. But as she reached the beginning of the heather covered hillside, China managed to snag her sweater sleeve on an old barbed wire fence. Donald took too long to untangle her, standing far too close.

'What are you smiling at?' she tested the water.

'You.' He couldn't resist. Leaning forward his lips were about to meet hers when Morgan barked impatiently and jumped up between them, splattering mud everywhere.

Laughing, they held hands tightly and forged their way up the hillside towards China's forgotten home. Brushing her curls from her face, she shielded her eyes with one hand and stared up at the edifice that crowned the island. Now just visible amongst the woods, it seemed like a ruined castle from a fairy tale, that great grey block of a building with its four impossibly tall chimney stacks, known locally as the Grange, built and first owned by the Laird of the island back in 1732. From that day it had always stayed in the hands of the Stuart family.

'The trees are a lot larger and closer than I remember,' she said.

'You've been gone a good while,' he came back, with just a hint of bitterness catching his voice. Finding what was left of the old hill path, they approached her late Aunt's house, both falling into silence.

China hung on tight to Donald's hand, suddenly feeling a little afraid. This was where the memories lived. The good ones and the bad. Up close, the house was in a worse state of repair than she had expected. The path directly to the front door was overgrown by spiky bushes, and sprouts of vegetation were peeking out of the crumbling gutters. Its dark slate roof had one or two obvious holes and there were broken fragments of slate scattered over the flagged path. Grimy glass rattled in rotting window frames as she took out the key that had been sent to her solicitors. When she opened the massive front door, the handle came off in her hand.

'That says it all,' she sighed, her usual clumsiness striking again.

Morgan barked once and squeezed his way in to the gloomy house.

Reluctantly, China followed, Donald letting her go in on her own.

It was the smell she remembered first as she stepped into the hall of the Grange. Even empty, there was still a hint of homemade pies and fresh laundry despite overtones of damp and mildew — at least there was to her. The old house seemed to whisper to the city girl, telling her ancient tales of its life, forgotten stories of her own. Morgan was obviously pleased to be home, padding up and down the stairs, tail wagging frantically and that massive tongue lolling from one side of his mouth.

'Why did you leave here, Mum?' China asked the shadows.

'Because she hated this place,' replied Donald from behind her. 'Your mam was an outsider. She only came here to marry your da and when he died she couldn't leave the Isle fast enough, as if she were afraid. That's what the gossips say.'

'How do you know all of this?' asked

China, suddenly angry that her mother had never told her anything about their life in the Outer Hebrides. Angry that she had died leaving things in such a mess. The old house groaned and creaked around them, as if in agreement.

'Your Aunt Beatrice told me some stuff. She said you'd be back some day and I was to tell you what you needed to know.'

'Why was my mother afraid?'

'Beatrice never mentioned why, as if it were a family secret. Maybe it was because she felt an outsider. The open skies worried her; she was never warm, Bee said, not even in summer,' Donald said, staring into her eyes. 'But you liked it, when you were a wee girl . . . you liked me . . . '

China stared at her old childhood playmate, forgotten memories of the two of them tumbling back. The helter-skelter runs down the bracken strewn paths that criss-crossed the island. Fishing off the pier with an old rod borrowed from Donald's dad. The roaring peat fires in wintertime and the first sight of the summer's butterflies, like moving carpets of colour.

A final kiss from that young boy as she had stepped onto the boat to the mainland, perhaps never to return. He had whispered something in her ear just before she left for that last time. What had he said?

Only then did China notice there was something crumpled up in the fisherman's hand. It rather spoiled the moment when she prized it loose. It was a 'Trespassers will be prosecuted' notice, with the black castle turret logo of the McKriven company all over it.

'This was on the gatepost. There are more of them along the fence. He's got a bloody cheek, with poor Beatrice not yet in her grave!'

The angry Donald was back again. China couldn't cope with him when he was like that. Back in Manchester she'd had one too many macho boyfriends who thought raising their voices and sometimes their fists solved every problem. She hadn't come all this way to fall for another man like that.

'You said Aunt Bea's solicitor could help,' she said, standing back a few paces, giving him space as she made the excuse of fussing Morgan.

Donald looked confused at her suddenly cool tone. 'Aye. He'll winkle out if Beatrice signed something she shouldn't have. I was over in Balivanich village this morning and told him about the letter. I hope that's okay.'

He could feel her growing cold and he wasn't sure what he'd done. After all these years apart it was so good to see her again, all grown up. He'd just hate it if he drove her away.

'Fine. I'm sure that will be okay. But you must have work to do. I'll have a bit of a look around and then lock up. See you later at the pub?'

'Sure. Can't waste all my day with a tourist, can I?' he snapped, totally misreading the situation. 'Be careful upstairs. There are a couple of ceilings down at the back where the roof's at its worst. See you later.' Before he said something he'd regret, he ducked through the front door and left her alone, his face a mask of suppressed anger.

Morgan barked once and ran round in a circle, eager to be off doing something, whilst China chewed at her thumbnail, wondering what had just gone wrong. But that was the chance she was taking — she didn't really know this Donald Dart. She had half forgotten childhood memories of a sweet young boy who was a large part of her early life, but maybe too many years had drifted by. The city girl and the island boy just didn't seem to have anything in common any more, except clouded memories.

For some reason she found herself crying as the dog whined around her, sensing her disappointment and confusion, and the house creaked and shuddered in the returning wind, as if it were trying to join in the conversation.

What had she been thinking — whirlwind romance? She was here to bury her Aunt and maybe it would be best to sell up to this McKriven company and get back to civilization as swiftly as possible. What was a pile of rotting old stones, a great smelly dog and this weather blasted island to her? But then her mother would have won. Having poisoned the childhood memories and put a barrier between herself and this wonderful place, she would have finally got her way. Somehow China had to get past this and work out what she really wanted from life. Whether she had really come home, or was only visiting a place she had long since outgrown.

There was a faint fluttering in front of her as China walked up the wide bare staircase to the first floor. She could hear a frantic beating of wings. In the tall arched window at the head of the stairs, she watched entranced as a single butterfly fluttered weakly against the windowpane.

It was still too cold for the island's

secret inhabitants to hatch from their chrysalises en mass, but within a couple of weeks the island would become covered in a variety of bright fluttering wings. This solitary butterfly must have hatched early within the slightly warmer environment of the house. As she held her hand up to try and capture the frantic insect, it settled on one finger, wings twitching nervously. For a second, she knew how it felt. Alone, confused, but fighting for a purpose in life. Then it was away, its wings flashing small beats of colour, flying deeper into her Aunt's house.

Her phone began to suddenly bleep in her coat pocket, breaking the spell, as a signal of sorts finally found its way through. Smiling at the six messages and four missed calls from Anthony's number, she wandered around the echoing house until she picked up a stronger signal then went to ring her friend so very far away in Manchester.

* * *

After she had finally spoken to a rather stand-offish Anthony for all of three minutes before the signal went again, China spent almost two hours exploring the Grange, glad of Morgan's company in those dimly lit rooms. Work suddenly seemed another universe away, all the gossip and who had said what to whom now strangely unreal. All that seemed to exist at the moment was this house, the sky and the sound of the sea.

Then there was Donald, of course. Where did he fit into the puzzle? At that moment she had absolutely no idea.

She was saddened by the decay permeating the house. Peeling wallpaper and mildewed plaster overlaying her bright childhood memories of the place. Most of the furniture had already gone. The solicitor had warned her about this, as Aunt Bea had sold most of her possessions down the fallow years to pay for structural repairs on the Grange.

But one room on the second floor

held a certain timeless magic. Aunt Beatrice's bedroom was just how she remembered it; a little faded and threadbare around the edges, but still alive with an otherworldly charm. Like a child who had sneaked into her parent's room, China wandered around as quiet as a mouse, peeping into lace lined drawers here and opening creaking cupboard doors there.

On the ornate dressing table, laid next to a silver hand mirror and a fine brush was a large green book in pride of place. As China touched the wisps of fine white hair caught up in the brush, her hand strayed to the book, wondering what it could contain. But then the feeling that her Aunt were still alive in this house and would return at any moment stopped her from opening it. It felt too much like prying.

Morgan flopped onto the massive four-poster bed with its carved stanchions and heavy head and footboards, turned around three times, then settled down for a snooze.

'Dog! Morgan, whatever! Come off there now!' China hissed at the mutt. Morgan opened his eyes, giving his new mistress a hang-dog look. He let out a tiny whine, such a little noise from such a large animal.

Then China realised something — this was his old mistress's room. It must still resonate with her presence, re-minding the faithful hound that she had disappeared somewhere. What animals understood of death was a mystery, but Morgan knew something traumatic had happened. Coming back here must have reminded him of what he once had.

Ruffling the crown of his head and pulling at his ears, China perched on the end of the bed and tried to comfort the animal. 'I know, boy. You knew her better than anyone else. This must be so confusing for you.' As the dog fell into an instant deep sleep, China was almost tempted to snuggle up beside him. She remembered the distant times when she had clambered into this very bed and listened to her Aunt's lilting voice as the old lady told her stories about the Grange and the whole Stuart clan.

In China's memories, it was as if Bea had always been an old lady. But a cluster of ornate framed family photos displayed around her antique dressing table showed a pair of laughing-eyed sisters dressed in old fashioned clothes, both in their late teens. It must have been of her Aunt and the grandma she never knew, Cora Stuart. Probably caused by the dust in that old room, she suddenly felt a tear trickle down her face again, which she hastily whipped away with her sleeve.

This trip into her past was proving harder than she had ever imagined.

Leaving Morgan to rest, she crept around the rest of the upper floor, peering into darkened rooms to see what else she could find. Again, most were stripped bare, even of carpets. Ivy had grown up the Western wall over the years, obscuring many of the rooms' windows, so it was a twilight world the city girl explored.

As Donald had warned her, several rooms had sagging stained ceilings and in two cases the plaster had collapsed, showing the broken wooden laths that had held the lime based plaster, looking up into the attic space and to chinks of daylight beyond that, revealing gaps in the roof slates that had let in the wind and the rain.

Through the cleaner windows China could see scaffolding erected at the back of the house. From what Skipper Dart had said the previous day, she guessed that was Donald's work, trying to repair the roof before any more weather damage was done.

Just for a second she recalled one of her favorite films, *The Money Pit*, with Tom Hanks and Shelley Long as a young and upcoming couple who were duped into buying an old mansion that was literally falling to bits. To turn back the clock and rebuild it took every penny they had, and it nearly cost them their marriage.

She shook the thoughts out of her head. This was her inheritance. She was the last blood descendant from the Stuart Laird who built the place with its four proud chimney stacks. After the funeral she'd have a proper word with Donald and any professional builders that lived on the island that could give her a ball-park quote on how much money she might expect to pay to return the Grange to its former glory. Over the years she had been quite frugal with her money, something she had inherited from her late mother, although she'd never admit it. It had occurred to her when Donald had led her hand-in-hand up the hill, what a magnificent hotel the place would make; breathing life back into all those rooms and providing the estate with an income so as it would never fall into disrepair again.

But she was no fool. The structure might be too far gone and selling it on or — perish the thought — having it demolished might be the only way forward. As she finally left the Grange with one long, backward look, Morgan now full of beans again after his dog-nap, first thoughts about possible heritage grants crossed her mind. There had to be a way to save the place, there just had to be, whether she stayed on the island or not.

That thought stopped her in her tracks. As things stood, she had taken a week's holiday to come to Butterfly Island and sort out her Aunt's estate. She had another week and a half left to use if necessary, but then that was it — back to Manchester, her cozy flat in a reclaimed city-centre factory, her high-flying job and her money-mad friends. Yet here she was, seriously considering the alternative of staying.

'Let's find you a big stick to chase, Morgan,' she said. The dog obviously understood every word she said, as he went ballistic, leaping around the heather strewn hillside.

Anything to take her mind off things. But the gentle wind blew the smell of the sea through her and the idea wouldn't go away. To have a real home rather than a shoe-box in a city full of strangers. There was a smile creeping across her face at the mere thought of that idea and it wouldn't go away.

3

On the adjacent hill to the woods that camouflaged the Grange, someone was watching China Stuart as she played with the massive Irish wolfhound beneath the clear blue skies. Someone with a pair of rather expensive, high-powered binoculars. James McKriven was not an unattractive man. In his late thirties he had kept off the drink, unlike his infamous father, and quietly turned the family firm, Na h-Eileanan Siar Property Developers into a modern, highly profitable company. Life in the Outer Hebrides was not impervious to change. The Credit Crunch and increasingly tough EEC fishing regulations meant that houses and land were constantly coming on the open market as local families struggled to make a living. Whenever that happened, James was usually first in the queue to snap them up at a bargain basement price.

Dark haired, dark eyed and dressed in a thick Shetland wool coat of deepest green, the businessman lowered his binoculars and watched the woman and her dog frolicking far in the distance. 'Well, those trespasser posters were a waste of time,' he said to the elements, and a small, well-rounded man wearing large spectacles who was shivering next to him. The two spies were half protected from the wind by a thicket of gorse bushes and last year's brittle brown ferns. 'Anyone would think she owns the place,' he added, poker-faced.

'Well, she does, doesn't she?' squeaked the nervous crony by his side.

McKriven cast his eyes to the heavens. 'That was a joke, Martin. Just because I was born on this lump of rock doesn't mean I can't crack a few funnies every now and again!'

Martin Japes, James's limp wristed right hand man laughed, a little too late. The business man shook his head in despair. 'You just can't get the staff these days. Pack up and lets get back to the boat. We'll let Miss Stuart get through the funeral tomorrow then we'll put the thumb-screws on her. How did Beatrice's solicitor find her heir? I thought we were home and dry with this one.' He watched for a few minutes more. 'Rather fetching though, our Miss Stuart. Maybe there's more than one way to skin this cat.'

* * *

It was half past twelve by the time China and Morgan returned to the heart of the island, hunger bringing them home to that cluster of cottages and buildings hugging the jetty. Of the three fishing boats owned by the islanders, only one was moored at that time; a small trawler with the lively name of the Daisy-Jane. In the bright midday sun, China managed to take in details of the wharf-front that she had missed the previous evening.

The two massive boathouses off to one side of the jetty were a complete eyesore, rather ruining the picture postcard view of the hamlet by the sea. Great rusted sheets of corrugated iron, repaired many times, over metal and timber frames long past their sell-by dates. Around them came all the clutter of an old boat yard. Nestled amongst the higgledy-piggledy stone built cottages with their gently smoking chimneys was the island's main shop. Its window frames and the front door glistening a bright red, it bore the legend, 'Bellamy's General Store' hand painted in brash colours.

The bairns were playing out again as it was dinnertime around the island. China played tug-o-war with Morgan and half a tree branch as they wandered lazily back to the Inn. This time the children didn't run away. One little girl with bright red hair actually gave the stranger a shy wave before her playmates grabbed hold of her and the pack of them scampered back to what must have been a small school, set further up the hillside.

Leaning next to the pub was one of the smallest, prettiest cottages China had ever seen. Sadly, its windows were boarded up, a familiar sign of the times. The dreamer inside of her wondered vaguely how much a property like that might cost. As the city girl pushed her way through the pub door, becoming entangled with Morgan as usual, there was a bowl of steaming hot stew and a chunk of crusty bread already waiting for her at the bar. The place was empty except for Mrs Baxter, her usual customers obviously taking advantage of the good weather and getting some work done.

'How do you do that?' China asked, hanging up her coat and scarf, looking forward to her much anticipated dinner.

Mrs Baxter smiled as she polished the bar's glasses. 'I saw you through the scullery window coming down the hill. I've always got something on the boil in my kitchen. Doesn't take a second to serve it out!'

'There's me thinking you were some sort of culinary sorceress.' Then China took her first mouthful of the mutton stew and closed her eyes. 'Correction. You are a sorceress. This is gorgeous!'

'I can give you the recipe if you like.'

'Oh, I'm more your can-opener-and-microwave sort of cook. If it involves chopping, measuring and mixing, I've never really got the hang of all that.'

'After the wake — if you've the time — I can give you a few basic tips.' There was a hidden question in that offer. Biddy Baxter was the eyes and ears of the island and she was digging a little to see how long their guest was planning on staying. Going silent for a while as she ate her stew, China picked up the unspoken enquiry. But it was one she didn't have an answer for herself — not at the moment.

'Wake . . . ? I never thought. Is all this costing you money, or should I be paying for that?'

Mrs Baxter coloured slightly, looking a little aggrieved. 'Heavens no, Miss Stuart! Beatrice left a tidy nest egg for her funeral. Me and her picked the buffet menu these five years ago when she first took to her bed.'

'Took to her . . . ? I never realized she had been so poorly for such a long while. Were you and her good friends?'

'Mmm . . . can't say Beatrice Stuart had what you might call friends. Acquaintances were about as far as she went. Enemies, she notched up by the dozen — a bit of a sharp tongue on her, had Bea. But she did love that great, stupid dog of hers, and I believe she had a soft spot for my nephew, Donald.' There was that twinkle in her eye again when she mentioned Donald's name. 'I should have mention it earlier, but if you want to see your Aunt before the funeral tomorrow, she's laid at rest in the Ice House about half a mile from here. It's a traditional place for the deceased to be laid out on the island — the name tells you why. Nesbit &

Sons from the mainland have done her proud.'

'Don't think me disrespectful, but I'd rather not,' said China, swallowing hard. 'I've some lovely memories of Aunt Bea from when I was a child. I'd rather leave them at that.'

'I understand,' said Mrs Baxter, softly, still polishing her glasses and sliding them precisely into their places on the bar shelves.

'I should really ring McGregor's the solicitor and get an update on what's going on. The Grange is in a terrible state. Hopefully my aunt left some money that can go towards restoring the building,' China tried to change the subject before an awkward silence settled between them. She had seen her mother's body before her funeral, and immediately wished she hadn't. For some people the experience was a chance to say a private goodbye, for others it marred the memories of that person when they were alive.

Mrs Baxter perked up again. 'That'll

be Douglas McGregor? He'll be in on the last boat this evening to pay his respects to Bea the 'morrow, so you can have a word with him then. Don't hold your breath waiting for him to show you a pot of money though. The Stuart coffers have been bare for many years. Your grandad Michael gambled most of it away.'

She glanced at Morgan who was chasing China's licked-clean bowl around the floor where she had placed it for him. 'You Stuart's have always had a love for the dogs. Some of the ones your grandfather put bets on are probably still running!'

Chuckling at Mrs Baxter's wry sense of humour, China caught sight of herself in the pub mirror. 'Look at my hair!' She sighed. 'Is there hot — '

'Water? The boiler's full of it, my dear. Help yourself.'

Leaving Morgan to make a nuisance of himself sniffing around the kitchen door, China finally got that bath she had been longing for since she had set foot on the island. Mrs Baxter's words about the pipes rang true as, whilst she was filling the massive four-legged tub with gallons of steaming hot water, they whistled an almost cheerful tune.

It seemed as if everything on Butterfly Island had seen better days. From the Grange down to the boat-sheds, the cottage next door and the various buildings on the wharf side — everything needed a large dose of TLC. Tons of Lovely Cash. As she lay there covered in suds, daydreaming about what she could make of the Grange if she won the lottery, it was as if the responsibilities of her ancestors for the welfare of West Uist and its people was seeping into her. She was the last of the Uist Stuarts. That was suddenly a heavy burden to bear which, up until 24 hours ago, she had never given a second thought to.

As the water began to go cold and the afternoon wore on, she finally had to leave the warmth of the tub and dry herself. Wrapped in a towel, she rummaged in one of her cases and extracted her trusty hair dryer. Well, at least I don't have to use a plug adaptor like you do when you go abroad, she thought absentmindedly as she hit the on switch.

There was an almighty bang and a blue flash arced from the wall socket to the plug on China's hair dryer. All the lights went out and the flex came away from the plug, smoke pouring from its charred end.

With a loud shriek, China shot out of her room and down the two flights of twisty, uneven stairs with the smouldering hairdryer still in her hand. That was how she found herself stood in just a very short towel, hair all over the place before various assembled islanders, including the solicitor Douglas McGregor, Mrs Baxter and, most mortifying of all, the Reverend Montgomery Fisher who had come to discuss the funeral service.

'Hi,' was all she could think to say. 'I think I've — '

'Blown something up?' Biddy Baxter finished for her, trying not to laugh.

★ ★ ★

'I am such a walking disaster,' China cringed half-an-hour later, as she sat, still with a towel wrapped around her wet hair, but at least fully dressed.

'I should have warned you, the electrics in this place were installed by Noah. No problem to fix though. Andy has been patching and repairing them for the last thirty years,' said Mrs Baxter sympathetically.

Andy turned out to be a tiny, wiry fifty-something Scot with a bush of white hair and skin like tanned leather. Handy Andy certainly lived up to his legend, as he seemed to be a man who could turn his hand to anything. In an isolated community, he was the kind of man everyone needed.

Picking up a freshly poured bottle of Clan Ale and one of Mrs Baxter's special three-tiered, door-stop sandwiches,

Andy nodded and winked at everyone, especially China, and ascended the stairs to do battle with the ancient wiring. Morgan, one eye on the sandwich and the other on Andy, quietly followed the man.

Whilst they sat in candlelight, even though it was mid-afternoon, China had a short conversation with all the people who had come to see her.

Her Aunt's solicitor, Mr McGregor confirmed what Mrs Baxter had insinuated. After a thorough investigation, he had found Aunt Bea had left only burial funds. In fact she owed about seven hundred pounds to various shops and local tradesmen, which he gently tried to break to China that she was now responsible for.

On the subject of the sale of land to the McKriven company, a document did seem to exist in the hands of James McKriven's solicitors, drawn up a few weeks before Beatrice's death, that had handed the whole of the Grange estate to the development company. Money had not exchanged hands due to her untimely death, and Mr McGregor felt sure the old lady hadn't signed the document without him as a witness. 'She might have been old, but when money was being discussed she was as sharp as a tack!' the solicitor smiled beneath his bristling old-style moustache.

The Reverend Fisher, fuelled by Mrs Baxter's best whisky, outlined a simple service outside the ancient Kirk high on the rugged cliffs overlooking Stuart Bay, weather permitting. 'The whole island will be there, as is tradition when a Stuart passes,' he explained, his pinched cheeks beginning to glow after the third whisky. 'Usually we get about a dozen people every Sunday, which is why I live on North Uist and the Kirk is empty during the week.'

'Do I owe you anything for this?' China asked, worried about the mounting debts in her Aunt's name.

'No, no, child. This was all part of the money she put away with Biddy's help.

Everything for the Service and the wake has been paid for. Give her her due; Beatrice Stuart was a stalwart church-goer. Even in her later years she was there in the Stuart's pew, front and centre. She even kept her old family bible there. It's still there undisturbed now, in front of her seat.'

'Well, at least I don't owe you anything,' China replied, a little relieved.

'Though donations to the Kirk restoration fund are always welcome,' smiled the Reverend, never one to miss a chance to rattle the plate. 'There have been some substantial movements in the building's foundations in recent years due to its proximity to the cliff.'

Just then the pub lights went on, rather ruining the Reverend Fisher's sales pitch, and a ragged cheer went up from the customers who had been sitting in the dark. As Handy Andy reappeared, Morgan watching him closely with a suspicious glare, he scribbled a bill out for Mrs Baxter on a page from a cheap notebook.

'Took a new bit of cable right back to that junction box I put in last winter. The bit of plastering will take a while to dry, that's all. When will you let me fix the rest of this place, Biddy? I'm rewiring it one socket at a time!'

'I'll let you know,' she fussed, fishing in her handbag for her purse.

'Hear that grunting? That'll be those pigs flying around Bellamy's General Store again,' the handyman replied sarcastically.

'Here, let me. It was my fault,' China butted in.

'I wouldn't dream of it!' Mrs Baxter began.

'How much?' China kidnapped the bill. Then she pulled a face. 'Do you take credit cards?'

'I'll do a cheque signed on the side of a cow as long as it doesn't bounce, hen,' said Andy, with a wink. 'Then again, me and the Stuarts have a patchy past when it comes to paying bills. Cash would do nicely!'

So, despite Mrs Baxter's protests,

China counted out eighty-five pounds into Andy's crinkly hand. 'Now that's the way I like to do business, Miss Stuart!' Then he was off like the wind, mammoth toolbox in hand. Morgan gave one of his quiet woofs, as if to see the man off, and stared hard at the pub door as it closed behind him.

'You really shouldn't have done that,' Mrs Baxter said, embarrassed.

'Call it a new tradition — a Stuart paying bills. Do you think it's safe for me to dry my hair now?'

4

Folk who wanted to attend Beatrice Stuart's funeral the next day were already gathering from the distant corners of Butterfly Island at The Cuckoo Inn, as the sun began its vibrant descent into the sea. Traditionally, no one locked their doors on West Uist. The island didn't even possess a policeman of its own, relying on a visiting officer twice a week from Benbecula in the tourist season.

It was an ancient tradition that, if a man were too far from his own house on a stormy night, he was welcome to walk in unannounced at any neighbour and be fed and provided with a bed or a couch for the night. So it wasn't uncommon for a person to come downstairs in the morning to find an unexpected guest cooking breakfast. This was just the way of the islands.

Tonight, Mrs Baxter was expecting to be making up at least a dozen beds on the pub benches for the extra visitors.

Already China noticed that, when she was in earshot the islanders switched from Gaelic to English out of respect. She suspected the ever resourceful Mrs Baxter of having had a word, but maybe being there for one whole day, she was now being regarded as less of a stranger.

As the pub continued to fill, she made herself useful by carrying trays of food back and forth and being introduced to families from far and wide. The landlady had called in favours from the local women, with several helping her in the kitchen and a rather sassy lady named Irene serving behind the bar. Morgan had stretched himself out like a slightly pungent hearth rug in front of the roaring log fire and was refusing to move — for even at this time of the year the nights could still be cold.

China was being shown how to work the hand pumps behind the bar when

Donald and his father came in. 'New staff, Biddy? Things must be looking up!' laughed Skipper Dart.

China grinned and held up a full pint of bubbles. 'I'm on trial and at this rate, I wouldn't employ me!' she joked about herself.

'Two pints — easy on the top,' said Donald. With a few whispered tips from Irene, China managed to pour two decent beers.

'Not bad,' John Dart said, holding his glass up to the light as the rich beer settled from swirls of cloudiness to a clear amber pint. 'Pay the lass,' he instructed his son, then went to join his cronies at one of the crowded tables in the snug.

'Thank you, sir,' China took Donald's money, wrestled with the old till for a moment or so, but managed to give him his correct change.

'Are you not having one yourself?' asked Donald, those gentle grey eyes melting her yet again.

'Well . . . am I? Where are we up to,

Donald? Am I just a bit of stuck-up city talent that you've got a bet on with your mates that you can bed me before I go back to Manchester, or are we something else?'

Donald took a deep drink before he answered. 'I'm not sure myself, China. Don't get me wrong — I'd never have a bet like that about you, or any woman for that matter. It's just we don't get to practice the social graces too often up here in the Hebrides. It's a hard life for hard people — but a good one. So I'll just ask how long are you planning on staying before I waste my time getting to know you all over again?'

It was at that point the city girl realised most of the other conversations around them had gone quiet. Chewing her bottom lip in confusion, she looked from one weather-beaten face to another, trying to find an answer from somewhere. 'I don't know,' she blurted out quickly, dropping the beer towel she had been worrying and running for the stairs. A second later, Morgan was on his feet and, with a glance in Donald's direction, padded after his new mistress.

'Don't bother to send off that application for guidance counsellor, son,' his father broke the silence with, and then everyone began to talk at once.

* * *

Alone in her room, now smelling of slightly damp plaster, but at least having a double socket that worked, China was determined not to cry. What was this with the tears all the time? Back in Manchester she had stood nose-to-nose with truculent bosses or bolshie work mates and given as good as she got. Something about the sea air turned her into a proper girl.

Morgan put his great untidy head on her lap and looked up at her with those sympathetic brown eyes, so she scratched his ears for him and calmed down. Picking up her phone from the dresser, she was surprised to find it registering three bars. Hitting fast dial, she rang Anthony's number, her usual shoulder to cry on.

'Who's this? Have you rung this number by mistake?'

'Stop being such a diva, Anthony. Can you talk?'

'It's Friday night, love. I'm on my third cocktail already. Tell your agony Anthony everything.'

So it all came tumbling out . . . her sudden feelings of responsibility for the Grange, the island and her confusion over Donald. Plus, she had the funeral to face the next day too.

'Donald Dart sounds like some of the pains I've gone out with,' advised Anthony, always known for wearing his heart on his sleeve. 'All bluster and prickly on the outside and a little squishy puppy on the inside. You've crashed in from the planet Venus, love. Disturbed his macho island-boy life and he doesn't know what the hell to do with you. Well, I'm sure I know what he'd like to do with you, but — '

'Anthony! We're not all like you!'

'Fair enough. He's not an angry man

without reason. You need to get him to talk, open up. Find out what's going on in that tartan heart of his. Best of luck, girlfriend — you're going to need it!'

'Thanks for the amateur psychology. Say 'hi' to everyone for me.'

'By that little phrase, I won't even bother to ask you when you're coming home — if you're coming home. And after you promised me, too!'

'That's the problem, Anthony. I have to decide where home is . . . bye . . . '

She hit the red phone symbol with her thumb and sat for a moment in deep contemplation. As usual, Anthony had sorted her head out for her.

'Come on, Morgan,' she said, fluffing her mass of curls that had dried by itself and touching up her lipstick. 'Let's see if that big lunk and I can have a conversation for more than ten minutes without one of us storming off.'

The dog bounced about, picking up her improved mood, hoping there would be some food involved in whatever China did next.

★ ★ ★

The pub was full when China made her entrance. There were a few glances in her direction, but thankfully not the attention she had expected. Slipping quietly behind the bar with Irene again, she busied herself with pulling pints and taking money, until the rush had died down.

Donald sat with his father and a few friends and either he hadn't noticed China had returned or he was ignoring her on purpose. Whilst the city girl helped bring in some of the glasses and the finished plates of food, Irene poured the pair of them a clear pint of Highland Lager.

'Staff break,' announced the pretty, rosy-faced woman with a shock of dark hair, streaked with just a few silver hairs. Taking their beer to the corridor leading from the kitchen, the two women clinked glasses and had a well earned drink.

'What do you do back in Manchester?' Irene asked.

'I sometimes wonder.' China shrugged,

licking the foam off her upper lip. 'I'm a PA for an advertising firm. Basically I organise stuff. You?'

'I'm West Uist's one and only teacher, half way up the hill there. I nurture them from three years old to sixteen. If anyone wants to take sixth form subjects they have to commute daily to Benbecula or work online — when that stupid mast of ours is working!'

China's attention wandered, as she glanced across to Donald.

'He's got you intrigued, hasn't he?' Irene brought her out of her trance.

'That obvious? I've just never come across a man with such contradicting moods. I've only been here five minutes and he's got me jumping through emotional hoops.'

'That's our Donald. I'll have to pass on commenting. We were engaged to be married three years back. He broke it off for no apparent reason. We're friends again now, but it's a small island and he's been out with most of the eligible girls around.'

China pulled an embarrassed face. 'Oh! I should have thought. Sorry.'

'What have you got to be sorry about? We lasses on West Uist have a theory about Donald; that he's waiting for the right woman to come along. Or that he's actually already met her and now won't settle for second best.' She finished her Lager with a flourish. 'You don't get a prize for being second best in this life, so I've been merrily getting on with mine.'

Her head buzzing with confusion about this contrary man, China busied herself cleaning glasses, trying not to look over at where Donald sat, before he made her jump with surprise by suddenly materialising next to her.

'My fault about before. Da says I'm a little too blunt at times.'

'You can say that again,' China replied once she'd calmed herself.

'We're away then. Get some sleep, it'll be a long day tomorrow.'

'I'll try. I'm beginning to understand the Stuarts used to be a big deal on this island. All I can tell you about how long I'm staying is — my boss back in Manchester willing — I'll be here until I've sorted out what's happening with the Grange. I suppose I'm going to have to see this villain of yours . . . McKriven, wasn't it?'

'That's him. You'll have a chance tomorrow, he'll be at the funeral, charming as you like. Don't sign anything he gives you, that's all I advise.'

China watched Donald go with his slightly tipsy father in tow. As he held the door open, she got a flash of that rare smile, as those weathered laughter lines highlighted his grey eyes. Like the little girl had done with her earlier that afternoon, she gave him a shy wave goodbye.

When the door swung shut behind him, she turned and nearly bumped into Irene. 'Don't mind me, China. As I said, we're just good friends now. I'm going out with someone on Benbecula now anyway — not as exciting as Donald, certainly not as volcanic, but he does me. You want to take on Mission Impossible, be my guest!'

The bar was officially closed, as much as it ever was. People were beginning to settle down for the night on their makeshift beds and China helped clean up before she said goodnight to Mrs Baxter, Irene and the rest of the volunteers, then headed upstairs for her own room.

Everything was whirling around in her head as she pulled the quilt tight under her chin, wondering if she was getting used to Morgan's distinctive smell or he was fretting less.

Tomorrow would be a big day. As she fell asleep she hoped she'd do her Aunt and the family she had never known proud. The wind was rising again as she found herself drifting off, to dream of holes in the roof, warnings from stern school teachers and Donald's laughing grey eyes.

5

The morning was upon her in a moment, as Mrs Baxter woke China at six and the Inn slowly came alive. For a few hours the snug might have been the back stage area of a play, as those who had stayed the night changed with a minimum amount of fuss into their funeral best that they had brought with them, and even more people began to call in to say their condolences to the last of the Uist Stuarts.

Dressed in a simple black dress she'd bought for the occasion, China shook hands, exchanged embraces and received and gave a hundred kisses. As the moving tide of people came and went, she was grateful that Irene had taken a shine to her and was constantly whispering names of who was related to who.

Mrs Baxter had been up since four, starting the preparations in the kitchen for the wake. Amidst the mourners all in their Sunday best, people were delivering trays full of pastries, a mountain of bread and various cooked meats plus all the trimmings. China was sure her poverty-stricken Aunt hadn't paid for all of this, but she decided asking Mrs Baxter about money again would have been taken as an insult.

Strangely, she felt calm in the eye of the storm. It was almost a detached sensation, as if she were still sitting upstairs in her room with Morgan cutting the circulation off in her legs with his immense weight, watching herself move through it all. If she had been asked to sum up the emotion she was feeling at that exact moment, she would have come back with, 'loved'. By tenuous ties she was related to most of these people who had gathered from all over the island and beyond. A great, supportive family that she never realised she had. It made her heart beat a little stronger at every touch, as if the funeral guests each transfused a little of their energy and strength into her, getting her through this sad day.

When the time came for her to walk around the hill to where the Kirk stood, that tiny stone built church too small to hold even a quarter of the mourners, she found Donald appearing at her side in a neat, if old-fashioned dark suit and tie, linking arms with her on the right hand side, and Mrs Baxter doing the same on her left. The sun was sparking off a relatively calm sea as a mild breeze stirred her mass of blond hair, the usually fickle curls tied back with a black ribbon and behaving themselves.

Over a hundred strong, the crowd of mourners was waiting outside the Kirk in relative silence. Even the children had been given a spit and polish then squeezed into their best clothes. Irene had charge of Morgan on a new black lead and he was sitting patiently waiting for all the people he loved.

More pleasantries were exchanged with the people who hadn't had time to call in to The Cuckoo earlier on. Then, carried on the breeze came the sound of gentle hoof beats. As one the crowd turned and looked down the stony track to see a pair of black horses resplendent in polished harness and tall black plumes on their heads pulling a black hearse, in which laid the small plain coffin of Aunt Beatrice. Leading them with his top hat tucked under his arm, dressed in Victorian funeral garb, was the serious-faced undertaker, presumably Nesbit or one of his sons.

Donald left her side on a nod from Mr Nesbit, as did three other younger men of the island. With practiced grace, they shouldered Beatrice Stuart's coffin and walked solemnly towards the Kirk's open door. In the mouth of the church, they balanced the coffin on a stand, where Reverend Fisher draped the simple wooden box with a rich tartan cloth, emblazoned in the centre with the Stuart emblem. An offshoot of the House of Stuart, the Stuarts of Uist shield contained a red Lion Rampant on a blue background above a green

Rowan tree, which grew profusely around the island.

With a brief smile to the gathered crowd, the Reverend stood behind the draped coffin with one hand touching the shield. 'Gathered family and friends,' he began. 'We are gathered here today in the sight of God to commit the soul of our sister, Beatrice Victoria Stuart into his arms, and place her earthly body into the ground . . . '

* * *

The service went by in a blur, and more than once China reached for Donald's hand and he gave it a squeeze of reassurance. Having watched the tiny coffin being lowered into the grave, she found the mass of the assembled mourners a little too much, and escaped into the cool solitude of the stone Kirk.

The church had stood on the edge of the cliffs since the 14th century, when China's ancestors first settled on the rocky island, stranded between the Inner and the Outer Hebrides. Out here on the tongue of land it had withstood the battering of the elements, much as the Grange up on the hill had, since the day it was built. Never having had electricity, there was a cold atmosphere inside its small knave. Only six rows of dark wooden pews lined the two sides of the church, with a small alter at the front.

As if guided by invisible hands, the city girl walked to the front row, where a faded carved Stuart shield was inlaid into the left-hand shelf. On the bench was an old faded maroon cushion, still indented as if the visitor had only just got up and left the Kirk. Before the cushion, sat on the heavy oak shelf was a small black covered bible. Daring to sit on her Aunt's cushion, China reached forward and touched the leather bound book, not wanting to disturb it on the shelf. It was as if the past was suddenly linked with the present. Coming from a generation that had all but abandoned the church, China had no pretentions that she was religious. But as she touched her Aunt's bible, a shiver went down her arm, just for a second.

'I used to bring her here every Sunday, as regular as clockwork, and most days of the week too,' said Douglas, slipping into the bare wooden bench next to her. 'She would lecture me on why I never stayed for the service all the way down in the horse and buggy, then moan all the way back about Reverend Fisher's posh Edinburgh accent and how the day's sermon had been rubbish,' said Donald, sitting down beside her.

'I just remember the stories she used to spin to me as a child . . . She seemed to be a lot happier person in my memory.'

'Thirty years ago she was. Living in that windswept house up on the hill blew the life out of her. In her last years nothing seemed to give her any pleasure. My Aunt Biddy used to take her meals up the path every day and they were always too hot, too cold, too salty or too large a portion. People stopped visiting her because she usually sent them home with a flea in their ear about something and nothing. Then McKriven started to visit her over the last few months . . . filling her head with nonsense.'

'Like what?'

'Money making schemes to save the Grange. Investments I suppose; she told no one, not even her solicitor. That's when the thief tried to trick her into signing the Grange away, I suppose. But without seeing this document, we have no idea how legal it is.'

'Oh, it's totally legal, I can assure you,' came a sarcastic voice from the back of the church.

Both of them turned around to see the immaculately dressed James McKriven standing in the open doorway, looking around the ancient Kirk as if there was a bad smell under his nose.

'Good grief . . . It's been a while

since I was in here. The place looks even more decrepit with the passing years.' He advanced on China, one gloved hand outstretched, a charming smile on his roguish face.

'Apologies that we haven't met sooner, my dear. James McKriven, at your service. And I honestly mean that. During your short stay on this little island, please do not hesitate to contact me for any reason at all.'

As China accepted the man's hand, she felt Donald tensing up beside her. Oh, please . . . don't kick off in here of all places, she thought grimly. But Donald Dart was trying his best to keep his temper.

'The vulture has landed, I see. Couldn't you wait until we see the poor woman off, McKriven?' He stood up in a fluster, fists clenched. The object of his rage hardly seemed phased.

'You forget, I was born on the island too, Donald. It's my duty to see a such a popular and well-loved Stuart into the grave with my respects.'

'Well I hope they counted the rings on her fingers if you went anywhere near the coffin!'

The two squared off against each other, China caught in the middle.

'I may be the atheist tourist here, but can we take the macho posturing outside, gentlemen? Your timing sucks!'

Both men seemed to hold themselves in check. It was Donald that muttered something about checking how his father was, exiting swiftly and loosening his tie as he went, his face like thunder.

'Always had a short fuse, our Donald,' James preened, taking China's arm. 'Let's walk a while and I'll let you catch up with the story so far concerning the Grange.'

They exited via a small side door that took them into the older part of the graveyard that surrounded the Kirk on three sides. Amidst small twisted Yew trees, the ancient grave stones were leaning at all angles, some of them completely flat, all covered in dark green lichen and moss. There was an odd calm behind the shelter of the church, broken only by the crashing of the waves somewhere over the lip of the cliff.

Barely thirty feet from the Kirk, a safety fence with yellow and black warning tape intertwined between the red plastic mesh staggered like a drunk on a Friday night along the cliff edge. As they talked, James McKiven walked them slowly towards the sound of the crashing sea.

'Back in 1997 your Aunt made a new will in a fit of depression, leaving the entire Stuart estate and the Grange in trust to the islanders. As far as she was concerned, her nephew had died at sea and you and your mother had vanished to the mainland, never to be seen again.'

'I remember we moved about a lot after we left the island. Glasgow, Dundee . . . then slowly further south. Lots of places. Lots of little flats and pokey boarding houses, that's all I remember.'

'Well, if your mother had wanted to hide your trail, she did her job well. I understand Beatrice had people looking for you both for some time, before illness and infirmity took her. So, in her despair she made that stupid will. But whilst I was recently conducting a general survey of all property on the island, your Aunt and I renewed our old acquaintance. After extensive research I produced a portfolio of investments that would benefit Beatrice and the island far better than her original will would, and she agreed to the wording of the initial document about six weeks ago.'

'So that's it then? The Grange passes over to your company?'

A vexed look crossed James McKriven's handsome face just for a moment, then he regained his debonair composure. 'Would life were that simple, China . . . I may call you China, I hope. For between us, without the interference of these inbred residents I'm sure we can come up with a sound business solution that will benefit all sides.'

'Let's hope so.' China was a little wary of this fox. She'd worked with many businessmen just like him in Manchester. But so far, he seemed to be making sense.

'In the small print of my company's contract with your aunt, she insisted on inserting a clause that stated that, in the possibility of any living relatives being found before the burial of said Beatrice Victoria Stuart, the deciding signature passed to that descendant. In short my dear — you.' It was then that McKriven overplayed his hand. The look he gave China was like a fox might give a chicken: hungry.

'There is one final twist to this tale, but I've my doubts that it's true. Seemingly two nights before her death your Aunt had a complete change of heart. Calling that wretched landlady of the Inn up to the Grange late at night, she wrote out a new simple will, leaving all her worldly possessions to you by name. Somehow, by divine intervention or otherwise, she had discovered that you were still alive.'

They were standing near the lip of the cliff at that point, the waves now visible some hundred feet below, smashing against the jagged rocks. James McKriven drew China close to him, his arm around her waist, under the pretence of keeping her safe.

'There was only an original draft of this fictitious will, which was never seen by her solicitor. It was witnessed by Biddy Baxter and she is the only person who claims it exists. Since that night, no one has seen the damn thing, despite a thorough search. Very thorough, I can assure you. So there you have it. Do you want to look through my business proposal, or shall we all scrabble around some more looking under every rock on the tedious island for this imaginary will? Your choice.'

'I'll have to think,' China gasped, breathlessly, pulling away from James. As she did so, her foot slipped and several stones clattered away under the safety fence, down into oblivion below. Moving quickly, McKriven caught her by one arm, moving the two of them away from the cliff edge.

'You do that, my dear. But careful now, this cliff has been slipping away inch by inch every year. We don't want you having an accident, do we?' And there was that predator smile again. It was at that point that China realised that James McKriven was a very charming, very ruthless man.

6

When China Stuart and James McKriven walked around the front of the Kirk, she was a little flushed and he looked triumphant. Most of the mourners had already set off down the path back to the jetty and the hospitality of The Cuckoo. Still looking daggers at his rival, Donald was waiting for China by the graveside.

'I'll catch you at the wake. I've a few business calls to make, reception willing. Take care now,' said McKriven.

'What lies has that scunner been telling you?' Donald blurted out before China could say anything.

'About missing wills and unsigned contracts. Why didn't Mrs Baxter mention this lost will, Donald?'

'Because she isn't a vampire like him. Once the wake was over and we'd given Bea a grand island send-off, she was going to sit you down in the morning and explain what had happened. I can presume McKriven hasn't found the will or else he'd be crowing about it. If he gets his claws on that piece of paper, it will go up in flames!'

'He's a bit of a shark, I'll give you that, but what have you got against progress, Donald? From what I've seen, everywhere on this island needs money pumping into it. Maybe selling off some of the land to McKriven will give everyone some much needed funds!'

Donald was beginning to come to the boil, she could see that again. The man spent all his working life at sea, and when cornered in an argument, he became a little confused with his words. But this time, China was determined to talk this problem through like adults, without her bursting into tears or him storming off in a huff.

'He's a crook! His whole family are crooks! Even at school he used to wave his money about, and — '

'Ah, maybe this is the problem — McKriven's money. He's flash, I'll give him that, but you've got twice his courage doing your job and three times his good looks!' Before Donald could reach boiling point, the city girl did the only thing she could think of to shut him up. She flung her arms around his neck, standing on her tiptoes, and kissed him soundly!

When the two of them surfaced for air, the fisherman was speechless.

Hooking his arm with both of hers, China towed him towards the path with an impish grin on her face. 'Now I've got the measure of you, Donald Dart! You start your arm-waving and that vein on your head standing out and that's what I'll have to do from now on! Call it physical therapy. So let's get to this wake before the wind picks up again and see if we can get to the end of a single conversation!'

★ ★ ★

The wake was already in full swing when the two old friends burst through the door.

'There she is! What have you been doing with the last of the Stuart's, Donald, you lucky lad?' cried Handy Andy, sloshing half his pint over several other mourners.

'He has been a perfect gentleman and escorted me back from the Kirk. A person could get lost on this island,' China came back with, before Donald started to stutter.

'Aye, I've heard that one before,' the handyman chuckled, but turned his attention back to the plate of food he had kidnapped.

Morgan was in his element, weaving between the full tables getting a titbit here and a snack there. When a morsel of food wasn't offered, he'd steal it from someone's plate when the owner wasn't looking. China pounced on the animal, roughing up his scruffy ears. He caught her a good few licks to the face in return.

'There you are, you rogue! Leave me to the mercies of the evil Baron McKriven whilst you're stuffing your face, as usual!' The dog gave her a puzzled look, then an abandoned chicken leg caught his eye and he was off in hot pursuit again.

'Like I said, Morgan is an eating machine,' laughed Donald.

As China went to grab an apron and make her way behind the bar, Irene Weise blocked her path. 'Not today, China. You're Bea's guest of honour. Her niece we all thought lost and now returned home.'

'Are you sure?' China smiled back.

'Are you?' the school teacher nodded meaningfully towards Donald who was embroiled in conversation with his father.

'Early days,' was all China would commit herself to. Taking an offered whisky, she suddenly found herself climbing up onto a vacant table so she could be seen. Sticking two fingers into the sides of her mouth, she let off a

88

ferocious whistle to gain everyone's attention. To help, Morgan barked three times, and the crowded pub silenced to a hush.

'I guess you know who I am. China Stuart, spirited away aged six. I've only been here five minutes, but I wish I'd had the sense to visit whilst my Aunt was alive and maybe it would have made the search for my past a little easier. But today is Aunt Bea's day. I want you to sit me down with a drink in my hand and tell me your stories of her life. The good with the bad!' She got a little appreciative laugh for that part. 'So please raise your glasses and join me in a toast. To Beatrice Victoria Stuart; slàinte and a fond slàn leat. Thank you all and let's get this party started!'

There was a whoop with dozens of raised glasses chinked together, and someone started playing an accordion with great gusto. Lifting her off the table, Donald had her snatched away by Handy Andy for the first dance, where

China soon found out he could be a little too handy.

'Aren't you the linguist?' laughed Donald a little later.

'The internet's a wonderful thing. I hope I said, 'Good Health and a fond Goodbye' but who knows?'

'It was close enough. I could always give you a little private tuition.'

'I bet you say that to all your . . . ' China began to give the common reply, when she caught Irene watching them from behind the bar. 'Let's park that one there shall we. I need to do a bit of circulating.' She gave him a gentle kiss on the lips and they parted, but as she moved around the crowded room she knew his eyes were on her all the time.

Well this relationship was starting to go somewhere. How fast or how far they took it was still in the hands of fate.

Frustratingly, as the celebrations of her Aunt's life went on throughout the day and into the evening, Donald and China seemed to find themselves at opposite sides of the snug. Whenever they managed to make eye contact and nod towards a corner of the room, by the time one of them had weaved their way through the revelers the other had become embroiled in a new conversation with someone else. For a funeral, this was the wildest party China had ever attended.

She did get a moment or two to reflect on the seriousness of the occasion, as during a brief lull whilst some folk had wandered out to the jetty to take in the fresh air and others had escorted the smallest children up and down the line of stone cottages where they were spending the night, she found herself stood by the bar next to her Aunt's picture.

It had been a nice touch, placing a photo of Aunt Bea in her happier youth with a full glass of sherry next to it, as if she were watching the whole proceedings, approvingly or otherwise. Already stood there taking a breather from the kitchen was Mrs Baxter.

'I gather you had a word with James earlier, back at the Kirk,' the older woman opened the conversation with.

'True. He's a bit of a contradiction too. Charming one moment and more than a little bit threatening the next.'

'Always enjoyed playing the part did James. Him and Donald used to scrap like cat and dog when they were in the school up the hill, but there was a connection between the two of them. I wouldn't go as far as saying it was friendship, but there was an empathy between them.'

'So James comes from West Uist too?'

'Born and bred. When Ma and Da ran the Inn and I was a size ten — so that goes back a bit — James's father spent a good portion of his time propping up this bar. I'd like to think it wasn't just the ale that brought him through the door.' She took a sip of her drink, not looking at China but lost in her reflections. 'We always said James would either make a fine business man or a criminal. I suspect he's found a way of combining both.'

'He mentioned a new will Aunt Bea made a few days before she died?'

'Aye, for once he's telling the truth. I sat next to Beatrice propped up with pillows in that massive bed of hers as she wrote and dated it with her own hand, then I signed as a witness. But now it's gone as if it never existed. I know folk are whispering behind my back that maybe I made it up just to stop James, but I didn't. She wrote a new will leaving everything to you and that's a fact, so help me God.'

Biddy Baxter glanced across at China, her hazel flecked eyes and that homely, friendly face as serious as the city girl had ever seen them.

'Then all we've got to do is find it,' said China. Mrs Baxter nodded and seemed to unwind a touch.

'Both Douglas and James have been through the house from top to bottom — at separate times of course. We reckon James got hold of a key when he charmed Beatrice with his business ideas. All I could think of was maybe Bea wrote about making the will in her journal, but I haven't had the heart to go up to the Grange and read it since she passed.'

'A journal? I think I saw it in her room when Donald took me to the Grange yesterday. She was in her eighties and she kept a diary?'

'That's right. On the dressing table will be a large green covered book. Every year she wrote about the comings and goings of the island people, the changing of the seasons, the storms and the bright days. One book a year for as long as I can remember. You really need to have them, China my love, no matter what the fate of the Grange. They're a social and natural history of Butterfly Island as seen through her eyes. If you ever want to get to know your Aunt again, read those journals.'

'Butterfly Island — I thought only my dad called West Uist that!' exclaimed China, her eyes misting over for a moment.

'At this time of the year when the

various species of butterflies are ready to hatch, the name tends to be used more than you think. It's a hard life here on this lump of rock in the middle of the sea, but there's a little bit of the romantic in all of us when the butterflies swarm.'

She held the younger woman's arm for a second and gave it a squeeze. 'Well, I'd better get back to it. This crowd are like locusts when they get going. I'm glad you believe me about the will. It saddens me that some of my good friends and neighbours think I'm making it up just to cause mischief. You see, not everyone is in love with this island existence like my family and I. Some would like to take James's money and leave for the mainland to start a new life. So you just take care who you confide in. Please take care.' Then she was gone back into the heat of the kitchen, leaving China to ponder over what she had told her.

The object of Mrs Baxter's concern, James McKriven had kept a low profile during the wake, but he had slipped quietly amongst the crowd, shaking a few hands here and buying a round of drinks there. All the while keeping an eye on the city girl, trying to work out what best to do about her.

Another direct approach here would be foolish. Although he had his allies in the crowd, that big lump Donald was keeping a close eye on China too. Then, he always did have a soft spot for the girl when they were small. No, his next approach had to be more business-like and on a professional level. What little he had been able to find out about China Stuart was she was a 21st century city girl, with all the expectations and aspirations that created. Appeal to her monetary side and he felt he couldn't go wrong.

So it was whilst China was engaged in her deep conversation with Biddy Baxter that James made his next move, catching Irene the school teacher alone, sneaking a quick cigarette outside the bar.

'Here's trouble,' she scowled at him.

'Don't be like that, Irene. There was a time before you went out with Donald that we were attracted to each other.'

'The only thing that you love is money.'

'True. But it's time for you to earn your wages. Get close to the city girl; make friends with China Stuart and keep me informed what she's up to.'

'But I really do like her, you weasel, what have you got to worry about? She'll be up and gone in a week or two anyway — or is it this story about Biddy and the new will true?'

'Of course it isn't! The old woman's making it all up. But I want to hedge my bets with China.' From underneath his coat he produced a slim cardboard folder with his company's black castle logo on. 'When she's nursing a hangover tomorrow like the rest of these yokels, give her this. She'll see the sense in signing the agreements her aunt and I drew up.'

Reluctantly, Irene took the folder

from the man, looking at it as if it were a poisoned chalice. 'And if I don't?'

James McKriven leaned a little closer. 'You were the one desperate for a loan this time last year. 'The school will close!' you wailed at me. 'We need to modernize the classroom'. Then there was the new roof you needed for your cottage. We were best friends back then . . . '

'I should have never borrowed from you; what a bloody fool I was.' Then James silenced her with a kiss, as China had done with Donald a few hours before. But there was no tenderness in this embrace, no passion. Rather it was his mark on the school teacher that she was his. He owned her now.

'Just do as you're told and the repayments will remain low. Cross me and you'll be living in the open fields!' Then like the pantomime villain he was, James faded back into the crowd smiling back at Irene all the way.

Oblivious of McKriven's threats, China cornered McGregor the solicitor.

'Tell me the secret of how you found me — or else I'll ask you to dance!'

Douglas McGregor fiddled with his glasses, his mustache bristling, a little embarrassed by the pretty woman from the city. 'Total chance really,' he fished inside his tweed jacket for a moment and eventually produced a crumpled newspaper cutting. 'Remember this?'

It was a story cut from the Manchester Evening News about a month before, showing the gathered staff of Slater & Marsh Advertising Agency celebrating winning a large European contract. Tucked away at the back was a familiar face with a mass of curly blonde hair.

'I've had people looking for you for years. You don't remember me . . . I was twenty when you left the island, but I'll never forget the day when that bubbly blonde little girl and her sad looking mother left and never came back. The light went out of your aunt's life and she saw only the negative side of people from that day on. When I saw this picture, I knew it was you and three days before she died, I showed it to Beatrice. You should have seen her smile. I have my suspicions about what has kept you hidden away from us. But this picture slipped through, thank God.'

China beamed at him and kissed the solicitor on the end of the nose. 'Thanks for never stopping looking.'

'My pleasure, Miss Stuart. My pleasure,' said McGregor, as China was twirled away for yet another dance, and the Wake went on.

★ ★ ★

It was late that night when the most hardy of the mourners left The Cuckoo Inn and headed for home, torches flashing erratically in the dark. China had managed a wonderful tipsy smooch with Donald before his father literally dragged him away with a backward cry of, 'We've got to be up at five this morning to catch the tide!'

The fisherman left her arms with her heart begging for more of him, as the tiny hairs down the back of her arms stood on end and she hugged herself, watching him go. Probably for the best, she told herself unconvincingly. A drunken fumble was no way to start a proper relationship.

Mrs Baxter was already in her dressing gown as she shooed her helpers out of the pub and slipped the bolts home on the wide front door.

'I thought no one locked their doors on this island?' China teased.

'After a day like today, if there's alcohol about there are a few of our regular patrons who wouldn't think twice of slipping back in for a night cap once the lights are out!' She chuckled. 'We'll clear up in the morning. Get to bed, girl before you keel over.' So China did as she was told.

After a brief wrestle with Morgan for command of the bed, she slept a dreamless sleep, only colours and faint sounds filling her head.

She awoke in daylight with a raging thirst, and wandered bleary-eyed downstairs, dressed in her Simpson's night shirt, to find the pub almost back to its normal self.

'Ah, great, you're up. Breakfast will be just five minutes,' said the ever cheerful Mrs Baxter. Then she fired up a massive antique vacuum and drowned out China's words of protest that she should have got her up to help with the cleaning.

The vacuum did nothing to help China's headache, so she hunted out some fresh orange juice from one of the monster fridges in the kitchen and found some paracetamol waiting on the side. Allowing the medication to do its work, she marshalled her thoughts for the day ahead.

As well as talking until her throat was sore about her aunt's exploits going back to before she was born, China had done a bit of business too. It seemed to her that whatever happened with the Grange, if those roof repairs weren't completed in the next week or so, the damage might be irreversible. Especially when one of the local amateur meteorologists told her the island was expecting a massive storm that was coming in across the Atlantic in about three days.

So she had hired Handy Andy, an islander by the name of Daniel White who was an expert roofer, and a carpenter from the main islands over for the wake, Jackie Kolodzeijski. All three men had promised to meet her at the Grange at eleven the next day. Well it was nine-thirty now, so China had to get her act together if she was going to start this team moving.

One thing niggled at the back of her head. She hadn't had time to talk this through with Donald, and now he was out at sea with his father for the rest of the day. He had taken on all the desperate repairs on the Grange himself, and was making a good job of them. But he could only do this part-time and time was running out. She hoped he would see the sense of her emergency plan and not take things the wrong way.

The day was bright if not a touch cold as she finally bundled out of the pub, wrapped up warm in jumpers, jeans and gloves. One place that had caught her eye that she had not yet had time to explore was Bellamy's General Store. It seemed an oasis of light and fresh paint in the otherwise tired line of cottages that contained the Inn and the shop. Almost pushing her over, Morgan bounded off in search of adventure, or food, or both.

She had met Frank Bellamy, a rather excitable ruddy-faced little man with little hair and sporting wire framed glasses the previous evening. Frank hailed from Kent and had sunk all his savings in the store, hoping to make a country life for himself rather than working in investment banking as he had done for too many years. Only open a year, he was finding making a decent living a struggle. For when money was tight amongst the small population of the island, they just did without.

'I thought I'd have the monopoly, not to charge ridiculous prices but to come away with a bit of a profit, but a boat comes in three times a week that's a floating shop. Guess who owns the damn thing . . . James McKriven.' He had told her in the midst of the revelry and dancing. 'He undercuts me week on week. It's as though he'd be glad if I went out of business. I provide my friends and neighbours with far more things than he provides. The postal service, for example. That man's got a plan, China, you mark my words.'

As she winced against the brightness of the day and slipped on a pair of sunglasses, China tottered down the cinder track for her first visit to the general store. The bell tinkled cheerfully as she opened the bright red door and a wonder of delights greeted her. Everything from groceries, hardware and everyday supplies were hung, stacked and otherwise displayed in every available corner. Frank Bellamy had lovingly taken the classic corner shop of old and customized it for West Uist's fishermen. But the main reason for her visit stood in pride of place to one side of the main counter — an automated cash machine, in glorious red of course.

'China! How's my favourite Mancunian this fine morning?' enthused Frank, bustling out of the back of the store and giving her a large hug.

'Fragile, Frank. Little sea birds have got inside my head and are pecking their way out.' She gave Frank an extra squeeze before she let him go, then went to pat the red ATM. 'How's this beauty this morning. Working I hope?'

Frank laughed, 'And here's me thinking you were just after my body. Yes, the beast is working at the moment. Though the signal cuts out as often as the phones most days. Help yourself.'

So China did, drawing out as much as her allowance would let her, getting cash for her new team of builders. 'Brilliant. What's with this signal thing anyway? My phone couldn't find a single bar again this morning.'

'Unlike its owner last night,' joked the little man. 'It's that damn aerial, China. It was put up at the beginning of the digital age and now it's out of date and in the wrong place. There are several sites further round the hill where the satellite company have been dying to build a new one for years, but your dear Aunt Bea wouldn't give them permission. She was a little paranoid about rays going through her head and the like.'

'So you're on the side that wants to cover the hillside with technology and cheap bungalows?'

'Perish the thought. I left the south of England to escape that life. But someone has to do something or this community is in danger of dying out.' He crooked a finger, looked around conspiratorially, beckoning her closer. 'Of course you know what's driving McKriven in his bid to own the island?'

She shook her head to show she didn't, her unruly curls bouncing wildly.

'Oil,' he whispered hoarsely, as if the very word would cause the world to crumble. 'I've got it on good authority from my contacts in the City that two large companies are already surveying in the area. Years ago the oil trapped beneath the Minch, the Little Minch and the Sea of the Hebrides was way too expensive to get out. Times have changed and new technology has made it a possibility. I bet McKriven has in mind a massive housing and leisure complex for the island. Somewhere for the workers on the future oil rigs to live. A halfway point between the mainland and the outer oil fields. But the Grange, the whole Stuart clan owning most of the land, and the islanders are getting in the way.'

'As conspiracy theories go, that's right out there, Frank!'

'Trust me. It makes sense of all the

scrappy cottages McKriven's been buying up these last three years, so that the local families can't afford to live on their own island. All the loans he's given to other folk that if he called in would ruin them. If I go, if this store goes, they will be reliant on his damn boat and he can name his own prices for consumables.'

'Sounds like a plan,' she had to agree.

'An evil plan, if you ask me. And here's you like a young nymph appearing from the sea, probably with the fate of us all in your hands.'

China pulled a thoughtful face. Frank's wild ideas certainly added up. She really wanted to let him in on her own short-term plans for the Grange, risking her own money, but Mrs Baxter's words from the previous night came back to her. Trust no one. Besides, the first person she should be explaining her wild ideas to was Donald.

Whistling for Morgan, who had gone scrounging around the back of the cottages, she began the long hike up to the Grange, the fresh air blowing the residue of her hangover away. She reveled in the view, sights like a lone kestrel hovering in the air over the rock-strewn fields below, dotted with the odd farm house or cottage. The trees swaying on the crown of the hill, all but obscuring the Grange, except for its four chimney stacks — which were probably in urgent need of repairing too.

In her head she hoped she was not making a big mistake with putting money into the ancient building. In her heart it seemed the obvious choice. She loved the place already, the years since her sudden departure from the island melting away. Sooner rather than later she was going to have to ring work and extend her time off. Then would come the big decision, to stay or go.

That little life-changing event rather depended on a certain Mr Dart and how their rekindled friendship developed.

She was red-faced and out of breath

by the time she reached the path that lead through the wild trees and up to the Grange. Nothing had changed about the place since her last visit. The grey building still looked lost and in need of a little love. That, thought China, covers both of us. Her team-supreme was waiting for her, sat on a collapsed garden wall exchanging ribald jokes and sharing cigarettes.

'That will stunt your growth!' said China, pointing at the cigarettes.

'That's not what my misses says!' Handy Andy was back in a flash.

'You're married? Poor woman!' Which brought a guffaw from the two other men. As a group, China Stuart knew how to handle men, it was in the one-to-one department that she tended to struggle.

She outlined her vision. A quick, professional job to make the Grange water tight again, then time could be spent estimating what other jobs needed doing and how much it was going to cost. Hopefully by then the mysterious will would have materialized, or she'd have to take a serious look at what James McKriven had to offer. Handing out the cash convinced her three builders that she was serious.

'Young Donald's done a great job so far, and the scaffolding being in place is a grand start, but there are parts of that old roof just waiting to cave in,' confirmed Handy Andy.

'I've seen a couple of outbuildings that are overgrown and are a wreck, Miss Stuart. If we can cannibalize their roof slates that will save time and a lot of money,' said the tiler, Daniel White.

'I like that line of thinking. And for goodness sake, fellas, it's China. Miss Stuart makes me feel about fifty!'

'All I can say is, thanks for the work, M — China,' Jackie Kolodzeijski put in. 'It means I can spend more time with my girlfriend on West Uist.'

'Let's hope there'll be a lot more work on this project in the future. Long distance relationships are hard.'

'Even harder up in the Hebrides. It's not like I can hop on a bus to come and visit Irene, and I have to earn a living on the bigger islands.'

'Irene the school teacher? I know her, she seems nice.'

Kolodzeijski, a grand Scottish name of the Polish clan gave her a broad grin. 'She is nice, especially to me! Shall we get cracking, boys?'

Leaving the men to start work on the roof, rolling back the flapping sheets of blue plastic Donald had covered the worst of the leaks with, China resumed her exploration of the house with Morgan happy to amble through his old home by her side. This time she went straight to her Aunt's sizable bedroom on the second floor. Sure enough her memory had been correct, as there on the dressing table was the green covered book Mrs Baxter had mentioned; her aunt's current yearly journal.

Eagerly she turned the pages this time, admiring Beatrice's fine copperplate writing. There was time to read the rest of the journal later, first she had to check out if the landlady's theory was right, that Aunt Bea might have written about making the new will. The last page sat there, written right to the end. Excitedly she read the final paragraph; these were her aunt's words and life — could she get any closer than that?

I'm having second thoughts about James's offer. What made perfect sense a few weeks ago now seems far too altruistic for that rogue. There are things he's not telling me and I feel uncomfortable about the whole deal.

Great news! After all these years, Douglas McGregor has found a young woman named China Stuart living in Manchester. There can't be two women in the world called that, surely — God bless her poor mother for such a wonderful name. I've never given up hope of finding the two of them, even these last hard five years. It has been as if someone has been hiding them from me, for how can two people vanish in this, the information age?

Which all makes up my mind that I

need to draw up a new . . .

And there the page ended, in mid sentence. A new what, Aunt Bea? A new will? It's got to be! China could hardly conceal her excitement as she thumbed through the blank pages after those teasing words. But there was nothing else, not even an inkblot. This didn't make any sense, as the entry was made three days before her aunt's death, the day Douglas McGregor had shown Bea that newspaper clipping proving China Stuart was still alive.

On an impulse she ran her finger along the fold between the pages, finding a slight roughness in the glued spine. Someone had torn out at least two pages! Well, if that didn't prove the existence of the will, nothing would. Deciding to take the journal with her for safekeeping, China had a further look around the place, opening every cupboard in the room. Doors that she thought were just more wardrobe space revealed a marvelous surprise, as on tightly packed shelves were row upon row of green backed journals, all neatly labelled with the year on their spines.

Perspiring with sudden nerves, China ran her finger along the dates. Back and further back down the years to the time her mother took her away from the island and the pair of them seemingly vanished. Odd memories returned to her as she remembered going to Manchester University and then her first working years. Tax forms always being wrongly addressed or calling her Charlie or Cherrie. Mail always going astray, problems with anything she ever filled out that showed on data bases. She had always laughed at it all, calling it 'The Curse of China'. What if someone had been manipulating things behind the scenes?

But as she reached the year she and her mother vanished, there was a space in the tightly packed volumes. Three consecutive years were missing. Three years packed with all that vital information, hiding the secret of what made her mother flee Butterfly Island. She swore again, something that was becoming a bad habit, looking to see if the books had been misfiled. Looking a third time with no luck.

'McKriven . . . ' was the first word to manifest itself. Hiding the will's existence she could understand, but why would he be so cruel as to steal the records of her childhood? Picking out the few volumes that had to cover her birth, she packed them with the current journal safely in her backpack. Then with a heavy heart she went to see how the men were doing.

It was then that she heard raised voices from up on the scaffolding and came back to reality with a bump. That voice shouting down the rest belonged to Donald Dart, and he was not sounding very happy.

7

Exiting out of the back door of the square house took China into a battlefield. Handy Andy was squaring off against an enraged Donald whilst the other two builders shouted their encouragement from the safety of the scaffolding. The diminutive Andy was taunting a red-faced Donald, swinging practice punches all over the place, whilst the fisherman seemed to have reached that point where he was so angry he could no longer speak. Providence lent a hand in the shape of a large scruffy dog, as Morgan suddenly swept past China and planted two large paws on Handy Andy's chest. The odd-job man went down like a felled tree and the dog, having stopped the argument, sat on his wire-haired opponent.

Jackie and Daniel dissolved into fits

of laughter first, then China joined in and finally the confused and frustrated Donald.

'Honestly, I leave you boys alone for five minutes and it turns into the school playground all over again,' said China, still giggling at Andy's plight, as Morgan refused to shift.

'Donald got hold of the wrong end of the stick, as usual. He thought we were starting to tear the place down for McKriven. We told him we wouldn't touch work for that devil for love nor money,' Jackie explained, swinging down off the scaffolding.

'I . . . kind of over reacted,' added Donald sheepishly.

'You don't say? Morgan, leave our amateur boxer alone now.'

Obediently, Morgan trotted over to China's side and sat down, but he kept a suspicious eye on all parties concerned. The animal did not like fighting or aggression of any kind and would always step in to stop it. It was just his way, and after years of protecting Aunt

Beatrice he had already transferred his loyalty to China.

Calming everyone down, she explained her plan to Douglas. After taking it all in he begrudgingly agreed it was a damn good idea. The job had always been far too much for just one man anyway, and if he was honest he enjoyed working alongside the others. After much huffing and puffing, he helped Andy to his feet and gave him a bear hug by way of saying sorry. It was a man thing.

It never ceased to amaze China how men struggled to express their true feelings. Only the very centred and the gay, like her friend Anthony managed to connect to their inner selves. Then with Anthony, he usually went and spoiled things by going so over the top it was painful. She smiled for a moment, trying to imagine what Donald would think of Anthony — two totally different breeds of men. If she stayed here — big if, still — they would have to meet, even if she had to go back to Manchester and pack her friend in a box and post him to West Uist herself!

'So are we all happy, gentlemen?' she asked the team. There was a round of 'Ayes' and the work continued.

'You're paying for this out of your own pocket?' Donald asked as he changed into his working overalls in the dusty kitchen. China tried not to ogle as he stripped down to his boxer shorts, but failed miserably.

'To start with. I've had a few crazy ideas on how to raise some revenue if Aunt Bea really did leave nothing.' Then she told Donald about the missing pages in her aunt's journal and the mislaid volumes.

'I saw her reading those books constantly when I was here. Maybe they're in another room.'

'But if she was bedridden unless you carried her downstairs to ride in the buggy to church, or your aunt brought her meals, she had no means to leave her room.'

'Funny you should mention the Kirk. Even when she was at her worse, just a day before she died, she got me to take her to the church so she could say her prayers. Sat alone in that old freezing place in her pew as usual for almost an hour. I wouldn't be surprised if she had caught a chill there.'

'It probably didn't help. Am I okay to leave you in charge of this lot for a few hours. I have to get my laptop up and running and do a little research, if the wi-fi connection at Bellamy's is working.'

'What about?'

She tapped the side of her nose. 'All good stuff, Donald. Trust me.'

'I do,' he reached forward and pulled her too him. 'Out of everyone I've ever known, I trust you.' They kissed just once in the kitchen, before Morgan began a low growl and they had to put some air between them.

'Barmy dog! You'll have to learn the difference between violence and passion!' Morgan just wagged his tail and panted at her.

'Passion, eh? Is that what we've got,

wee China Stuart?' Donald said as he zipped up his overalls, ready to do some work.

'Getting there, if we can just find an off switch for that temper of yours. Why do you fly off the handle all the time? It's like being with a different person when you're like that.'

The fisherman seemed to think long and hard for a moment, as if he were wrestling with his inner demons. 'When I was a bairn, all I wanted to be was a fisherman like Da. He took me out to sea when I was three and I never wanted anything else. So I got my wish. The job is not what it used to be but we get by with reduced quotas and the like — just. But I remember being my happiest when I was running through the fields with a little wild haired girl holding onto my hand, as we scared up all the butterflies into the sky.'

'Like a living carpet,' she recalled, smiling at him.

'I wanted those days to last for ever, but they didn't. You went away and I didn't understand why. It was like a piece of me was missing as I grew up. Things I wanted to tell you at the end of the day that I never could. Conversations we never had. So I grew up resenting that you'd left me behind. After all these years, even after a few other relationships, I've still this ball of rage inside of me that I can't get out.'

There was a silence between them. China didn't know what to say.

'When you leave again . . . '

'If I leave . . . '

'If. Such a tiny word but full of hopes and promises. Like when you ask Da to do something and he says, 'later', you know later will never come.'

'Well 'if' is here now. I still don't know why my mother had to get away, to run. I always thought it was Aunt Bea's fault, that she hated Mum for living when her nephew, my dad Campbell Stuart, died. But the little bit I've just read in her journal seems to show she still had a great affection for Mum, that she wanted to find the two of us again. I have to put the past straight in my head before I can move forward, Donald, whether it's here or back in Manchester. Then we'll see where that passion can take us.'

He nodded, letting that sink in then went to join the others up on the scaffolding. Did he understand? Did she really understand? Life had taken one of its usual one-hundred-and-eighty degree turns and she hoped and prayed the pair of them would survive it.

Saying 'bye to the team, she let Morgan lead her back down the hill at a fair pace, as away on the horizon the sky was taking on a darker hue. Clouds were building up in the east and the storm, a few days off, was on its way.

⋆ ⋆ ⋆

Getting back to The Cuckoo Inn, China helped behind the bar while Mrs Baxter had a break, then she fed the ravenous wolfhound and finally she went back out to the wooden table and benches at the front of the pub with her laptop, pen and paper. She had set herself a task. Given one smallish island, what could be done to earn money from it? What sort of people would be interested in visiting the place. Wildlife enthusiasts? The sixteen different species of butterfly alone were of some value. Then there was the shark fishing, all manner of water-sports, these made a start. Given the right incentives what companies could be attracted to the island, raising the population, providing more jobs to keep the teenagers in work and halt the gradual migration of young families in search of work?

Then there was the historical value — the marshes to the west of the island had evidence of early human popula-tion as far back as four thousand years ago. The solitary standing stone on the peak of Aon hill; who had placed it there and why? Then the marvelous Grange itself on the taller Dhà hill and the Kirk out on the treacherous eastern cliffs.

Using the skills she had learned in the advertising agency and treating Butterfly Island like a marketable product, she began to formulate several avenues that were worth exploring. It was about then that Irene appeared at the table, with James McKriven's proposal folder in one hand.

Aunt Bea's funeral had been on a Friday, so today the school was closed and Irene had had time to recover from the wake. But the folder had sat there by her bed as her boyfriend Jackie had risen early to get ready to meet China up at the Grange as arranged.

'What's that doing here?' he had asked about the folder.

'Just something I said I'd do,' she'd replied from under the bed covers.

Irene had missed China by minutes that morning, and the folder was hidden under her coat whilst she helped Mrs Baxter with Saturday dinners in the pub. Having nodded to China as the city girl returned from the Grange to grab a sandwich, she eventually screwed up her courage to do McKriven's dirty work for him.

'Hi,' she smiled stiffly. 'How's the head?'

'Better than it was this morning,' China said, scribbling down another few notes. 'I met your Jackie today, he seems really nice.'

'He is, for putting up with me and my endless tales of which kid tried flushing our school newts down the loo this week. Did that job for him work out okay this morning?' China stopped writing, shut her laptop and explained the emergency plan to repair the roof of the Grange before the forecasted storm. 'Sounds a great idea. Plus I'll have Jackie to keep me warm for the next few nights — bonus!

Her enthusiasm for the new project to save the Grange bubbling up inside her, China was tempted to tell Irene a lot more. It was times like this she missed Anthony as her sounding board, but the mobile reception was still iffy. However there was something about the schoolteacher's manner and that ominous looking folder that put her on her guard.

'What's this then?' she finally said, nodding towards the folder.

'My pound of flesh,' Irene sighed, pushing the thing across the bleached wooden table so that it rested against her laptop. 'I promised James I'd show it to you. It's that not-so-secret proposal he made with Beatrice to buy a large chunk of Stuart land and what his plans for the Grange were.'

China opened it pensively. It was a complex document, with a DVD tucked inside the folder lip and the all important copy of the contract prepared for her aunt to sign. Only now he was after her signature, and using Irene as some sort of go-between.

'So Aunt Bea hadn't signed it after all. Good for her. It seems a heavy read. I don't feel comfortable looking at it without Mr McGregor with me.'

Irene held up her hands in agreement. 'I understand, I really do. I had a peep at it last night and it looked very complicated. Douglas McGregor's gone butterfly hunting for the day in the marshes; he'll be back when he's hungry. It's his passion and we lose him for days when he gets over to West Uist at this time of year.' She rose as if to leave, but China stopped her.

'Why are you being McKriven's messenger? I thought most of the islanders hated his guts?'

'They do. I do, but he'd been buying up old debts and creating new ones to curry friends, so certain people, like myself, are in his pocket. There, I've told you. Can't say I like it, but what options have I got?'

'The more I hear about James McKriven, the less I like him. It's as if he's playing chess with people's lives. All these tiny, secretive moves adding up to a very complicated, very lucrative end-game.'

'Who knows what goes on in that

head of his. Without boring you with the details, I'm not the only one who he's got over a financial barrel.'

Taking a big chance, China quietly told the school teacher about the missing pages in her aunt's journal.

'The swine! He's been spreading tattle-tales about Biddy Baxter, hinting that she's off her head and she imagined this missing will.' Irene was outraged, her beaten down demeanor now driven out by anger.

'I gathered as much. But what puzzles me is, if James had found the will he would have just destroyed it and never mentioned it again. The fact that he's going to all this trouble to convince people it doesn't exist, and that Mrs Baxter is lying suggests to me he hasn't found it at all. But where would my aunt have hidden it?' said China.

The two women batted ideas back and forth while the afternoon wore on. When the landlady brought them a couple of shandies to quench their thirst, Irene patted the bench seat next

131

to her. 'Just listen to this, Biddy. China, tell her about the missing pages.'

As China's tale unfolded, it was Mrs Baxter's turn to bristle with anger. 'I knew it. I knew that little beggar had a key. He must have searched that house top to bottom looking for that will, then when he couldn't find it, removed the one piece of evidence that proved it exists. I'll give him a piece of my mind when I next clap eyes on him!'

'Just keep this between ourselves. Knowledge is power, ladies! I've not even told Donald, he'd only go ballistic again anyway.'

'And how are you two getting along?' Mrs Baxter couldn't help asking.

'Okay. It's like talking to two different people at the moment. The eight-year-old inside of him still blames me for leaving him behind, even though the adult is beginning to realise I had absolutely nothing to do with the idea. After all, I was only six at the time! Mum told me we were going on an adventure holiday. I thought we'd be coming back after two weeks, but the holiday went on indefinitely and we constantly moved from here to there.'

'That must have been so confusing for you, love,' said Mrs Baxter.

'I suppose it was. It all seems so long ago now; it was just stuff that happened. But another thing I've already learned from Aunt Bea's journal — there was no argument there, not on her side at least.'

'That's right, love. All the time you were away, Beatrice never gave up hoping that the two of you might appear on a boat one day, returning home. She must have spent a small fortune down the years with McGregor trying to find out where you'd vanished to.'

'I wish, after Mum died . . . I wish I'd had the gumption to come in search of the truth and meet Bea again while she was still alive. I've enough stories about her from the wake to write a book, but I missed speaking to her.' She sighed and tried not to get upset again, but Mrs Baxter's gentle hands and Irene putting one arm around her shoulder started them all off crying.

It was a strange sight that met solicitor Douglas McGregor's eyes as he wandered down the track, nets and butterfly equipment in hand. Three women laughing and crying all at the same time. 'Place has gone mad,' he muttered to himself. 'Have you lot just kept drinking right through from yesterday, or is this a more general outbreak of hysteria?'

'Oh, get in the pub you insensitive man and I'll make you something to eat!' shouted Biddy, marching the baffled solicitor through the Inn door.

'What did I say?' he cried, much to China and Irene's amusement. James McKriven was right, the two women were becoming firm friends, but not in the way he intended. Irene had already decided she was not telling him a thing of their conversations, unless China wanted her to. The friends of

China Stuart were beginning to close ranks. Drawing strength from her leadership and guidance, McKriven was not going to have things all his own way as he had been used to for so long.

8

The next few days on Butterfly Island passed without any new revelations. Work on the Grange roof continued apace, with China making several more cash withdrawals from the general store's snazzy red ATM to pay for materials. Internal work such as replacing the fallen ceilings would have to wait until later, as the four men worked tirelessly to make the slate roof weatherproof once again.

On the Monday morning, with a lump in her throat and some of the island's butterflies in her stomach, she finally made a very important call to her boss back in Manchester. That done, China could concentrate on her plans for the future, contacting several sport and outdoor adventure companies to see what interest she could garner.

But of her aunt's new will, there was still no sign.

'Should you not sign James McKriven's business deal and Beatrice's new will never surfaces, that leaves us with her original wishes, to donate the Stuart lands to the island,' explained McGregor as all parties concerned gathered for a council of war on Monday evening in one corner of The Cuckoo Inn's snug by the crackling log fire. 'That sounds better than it should. When my predecessor made that first will for Beatrice it was a bit of a sloppy affair. He made no account of several of the listed beneficiaries dying before Beatrice and not leaving wills of their own. Nor that people would sell up or just move away. It's a sad fact that, if this first will applies, McKriven will own over 50 per cent of the disputed land, as he's picked up the pieces of the jigsaw down the last ten years for buttons. Without that missing will it's a case of heads he wins, tails we lose.'

There was a murmur of annoyance and disapproval from amongst the gathered friends.

'We've got no one but ourselves to blame. For years we've just let that devious swine play Monopoly with our island. This is our last chance to save it and ourselves. Thanks to China for giving us a bit of spirit and organization and having the faith to put her own money into rescuing the Grange,' said Donald. There followed a brief round of applause, much to the city girl's embarrassment. It took one single woof from Morgan to shut them all up.

'Thank you for gathering here today, loyal subjects and new friends,' China lightened the mood as she stood up in the centre of the people, never one to shy away from a product presentation. 'The problem: James McKriven. His plan: something big and nasty that will wreck the environment, destroy the local community and possibly turn this little island into something akin to McKrivenWorld. So, what can we do about it, then?'

'Get on with it!' heckled Handy Andy, only for Mrs Baxter to catch him a clout around the back of the head with a rolled up newspaper.

'My first decision has been not to sign the deal he nearly charmed Aunt Bea into taking. I've got to be honest, no matter what we all think of the man, he has put together a tempting portfolio. There are some genuinely good ideas to breathe new life into Butterfly Island. Just because of where they have come from shouldn't make us reject them out of hand.'

'You're not thinking of signing are you?' Donald butted in.

'Pass me that newspaper, Biddy,' sighed China. 'You're not listening are you, you great huggable man? I will not sign this deal. But pulled apart and cherry-picked for the most beneficial schemes to the islanders rather than McKriven's empire, there are a few damn good ideas hidden in there.'

'So where to next?' Irene asked, snuggling against her Jackie.

'Douglas here is going to bring the full power of the law to stop McKriven hassling me to sign. Also, we'll tie the first will up in probate to give us a bit of breathing space. I propose we set up a holding company, Butterfly Island Enterprises, to buy out any farmers in financial trouble before they are bullied into selling to the enemy and to bail out people who were already conned into his financial help schemes — '

'Like me,' Irene held up one reticent finger.

'Like our gullible schoolteacher here, and buy up their debt to stop McKriven piling on the interest. In short, we counter the enemy at every turn and claim this island back for its rightful owners: the islanders!'

As she got another rousing cheer, her mobile rang, making everyone jump. Holding up one hand for silence, the feisty blonde took the call.

'Shush! This will be our exclusive agent in Manchester. How's the hair, Anthony?' She let her best friend waffle on for a while until the pub crowd began to get restless. 'Anthony, pause for breath. Did we get the loan?' There was a moment's complete silence as she listened to the answer, hoping the reception wouldn't pack in like it usually did. China Stuart's fist suddenly shot into the air. 'We have got the initial loan from my old firm! Butterfly Island Enterprises is officially go!'

There were ecstatic hugs all round as China tried to say goodbye to her Manchester friend. 'You have just got to get yourself up here, Anthony . . . Well wear a hat if you're afraid the salt air will wreck your follicles! Just think of all these hunky fishermen waiting to meet you!'

When the chaos died down and the meeting broke up for a round of drinks, China perched herself on Donald's knee and gave him a hug. 'Small steps,' she said, grinning from ear to ear.

'What will you tackle first? Continue the work on the Grange?' he asked.

'No. I've got separate plans to fund that. And the new Boathouses, and the refurbishment of The Cuckoo.'

'Slow down, woman. You're on fire!' laughed the fisherman heartily.

'We're going to build a second pier out past the marshes. It will be the start of a sports centre and marina. The land is useless for farming out there and I'm told the scuba diving is best along those cliffs and the coves. A pier with a real road linked to this jetty. With the proper infrastructure in place we can attract several business ventures I've been courting the last few days.'

Donald looked at her as if he was seeing her for the first time. 'You really are serious about all this aren't you? You used the words, 'my old firm' just then. Am I to take it that you're staying?'

She smiled at his worried frown and kissed away the furrows on his forehead. 'That is a resounding yes, Donald. I've handed in my official notice taking holidays owed in lieu of notice. My flat is up for sale and I've burnt my bridges from my old life. Your wee China Stuart has come home.'

As he lifted her in the air and spun

her around, she was trying not to think of what might happen to spoil this moment. What angles she may have missed that McKriven might drive a wedge through to wreck their plans.

'Put me down, you big Scottish nutcase!' She laughed. Donald obeyed, all that old aggression noticeable by its absence. He was beginning to rediscover that he had a sense of humour. 'Answer me this. I remember walking hand in hand onto that stone jetty with my mum on that last day. Stupid here thought we were going on our holidays. Then you gave me a kiss and asked me something, or told me something. I can't quite remember. It all comes back to me in my dreams, but the words are just out of reach.'

Donald shook his head, determined not to spoil the moment by pushing his luck and telling her what he said. 'I can't really remember. It was probably something juvenile, like send me a post card, or the like.'

'No it wasn't. This was really

important. Think, damn your sexy grey eyes. Delve back into that seaweed clogged brain of yours.'

So complete was the crowd's bubble of happiness that they failed to notice the snake in the grass. Finishing his half of Lager, Martin Japes, McKriven's sidekick, scuttled out of the pub, hurrying back to the jetty where his master's boat was moored. The consequences of that oversight would begin to be felt the very next morning.

* * *

'Something's wrong,' China put her mobile down on the bar next to her half finished breakfast as Mrs Baxter came out of the kitchen. 'That was the Wildlife Conservation Society. They understand we're planning to look into putting a permanent track through the marshlands and would like to point out, before we waste any money or time, that there are at least a dozen protected species of newts and insects that by law must not be disturbed.'

'But you only told us that idea last night? How . . . ?'

'We might have a mole in our midst. Someone has run straight to McKriven with our ideas. Which means he knows about Butterfly Island Enterprises.' Her phone rang again, biting her bottom lip she thumbed it on.

'Calm down, Anthony! Deep breaths. Now begin at the beginning.'

Five minutes later, China's already pale complexion was two shades whiter. 'Oh, he's good, I'll give him that. Someone registered the name Butterfly Island Enterprises first thing this morning at Companies House before Anthony could get his act together. Plus, the bank has come back to my old boss to say there is a problem with my credit rating. It seems I owe money on lots of goods I've never seen or heard of, so naturally they are a little concerned about lending me any money.'

'James McKriven. I should have tanned that little brat's backside for him all those years ago . . . ' Mrs Baxter tailed off as the pub door swung open. In his expensive, spotless green coat, the very devil stood framed in the doorway enjoying the dramatic entrance.

'James. You've done this before, haven't you?' China smiled grimly, running her fingers through her curly hair. From out of nowhere, Morgan appeared and sat next to his mistress, leaning against her for support.

'Seen off wannabe opposition? Too right I have, wee China Stuart. I've more people in my pockets than you could ever imagine.' He sat on the bar stool next to China and smiled at the livid Mrs Baxter. 'And I could always outpace you when I was a bairn, Biddy. You were never built for running.'

'Why you cheeky — ' Mrs Baxter began, but China's raised hand stopped her in mid flow.

'Could you make us a coffee please, Biddy? Seems like it's time for a serious business talk.' With Mrs Baxter reluctantly out of earshot, China finished off her last piece of sausage, drained her coffee cup with a fresh one imminent and stared James McKriven out.

'It was all going so swimmingly before you returned from the dead — or at least the invisible. Do you know how much I've spent over the years keeping your identity a secret? All those screwed up tax bills? The misdirected mail? Your name erased from as many data bases as I could hack into? And you never had a clue why.'

'I'm the last of the Stuart line. If I hadn't existed, you'd have been home and free. Either the original will or your business proposal, it didn't matter. Butterfly Island was nearly yours.'

'Then that stupid old woman had second thoughts and went and died.'

'After making a new will.'

'Which doesn't exist.'

'Oh yes it does,' China replied sternly.

'Prove it,' McKriven glared back.

They sat in silence as Mrs Baxter brought in the coffees, paused only long enough to give James a hard stare and went back into the kitchen.

'I was going to look into the protected species angle before we put in any plans for the marsh track . . . '

James slipped a thin document across the table for her to see. It was a report about the indigenous wildlife of the island — independently commissioned of course.

'There before you again. I was just going to make the road, say 'oops' when another few useless insect sub-species went extinct and pay the fine. So much more cheaper.'

'It starts with insects, James, then it ends with islanders. But you don't differentiate between the two, do you? They're all in the way of James McKriven's progress.'

He smiled and nodded gently. 'You so 'get me' don't you? What a fabulous mind you've got inside that delightful little face. Both are wasted on that dullard, Donald. If you ever fancy coming over to the Dark Side, think of the team we would make.'

148

'Not a chance.'

The man drank his coffee, as Morgan decided it was time for him to go, the dog's hackles raised in a line down his back and that familiar low growl beginning to sound from the back of his throat. 'I'll be off then, to throw more penniless crofters out of their hovels. That offer of a partnership won't be open for ever. Until you say yes, or you limp back to Manchester with your tail between your legs, I'll be on your back every step of the way.'

China watched him go, with Morgan two steps behind him. Part of her wished the dog would give him a little nip, but then James would have taken great pleasure in reporting a savage dog attack and demanding that the beast was put down. He was taking no prisoners in this game. The man obviously had a fortune riding of whatever shady deals he had planned for this wonderful island.

She would just have to stop him, that was all.

'Some things have been rectified easily. We've registered the new company as Butterfly Island Sanctuary, using the wildlife angle. James kindly forgot the report he had paid for on the bar when he left, so I've had a long chat with the Wildlife Society and they're sending people to verify his findings. That way, we work in tandem with them when we get to the planning stage of things. To be honest, that had always been my intention anyway so Mr McKriven has simply sped that process up for us.'

This council of war included only China, Douglas McGregor the solicitor, Donald and Mrs Baxter, locked in the pub kitchen with the curtains drawn.

'Good. I've started trying to untangle your financial affairs, China, but as you can guess making a mess of something is far quicker than tidying it up,' said McGregor, fiddling nervously with his glasses. 'I had a word with your old boss, Mr Marsh. He's a very under-standing man. Out of his own pocket, he's willing to fund the provisional part of your plan, seeing as the banks won't play, but he wants a 20 per cent stake in the new company.'

'That's pretty fair under the circum-stances . . . Donald, what's wrong?'

Since the emergency meeting was called, the fisherman had shuffled about, totally distracted. 'Sorry, it's me. I feel so out of my depth with all this business talk. When you get going you're like a different person, China. I know we've talked about my temper and all my — what was it? — anger management issues. But in a case like this what I really need to do is find James McKriven and give him a damn good thumping!'

'And I'll hold your coat, love,' agreed Mrs Baxter.

'That's why he appears like Dracula out of the mist when you're not here. He's a back-stabber, not a fighter. We resort to those tactics and the law will get dragged into it. I suspect inside one of those many pockets James was alluding to, he's got at least one mid-ranking policemen on the McKriven payroll.'

Donald, obviously not satisfied with that answer, was about to say something else when the pub door suddenly flew open. It was Jackie Kolodziejski, with blood over his face and hands. 'There's been a bad accident up at the Grange. Andy's got a broken leg at the very least and Daniel's twisted his ankle,' he gasped.

'What happened, man?' Donald grasped his friend's shoulder, concern etched all over his face.

'It was the scaffolding . . . it just collapsed like a load of drinking straws! I think someone went up there last night and was messing with it.'

By the terrible look on Donald's face, they all knew who that would be. Things were getting deadly serious.

As Jackie ran back to the school to get Irene, the island's official First Aid person, Mrs Baxter rang through to the mainland to summon a real doctor.

'It's all going wrong. This is my fault, I didn't treat James as a serious threat,' China said. She felt cold and scared at the thought that Donald could have been up on that roof when the scaffolding fell apart. But when she turned and looked for her man for some comfort, he was already gone.

The chilled wind whipped at her flimsy top as she ran outside and looked frantically around. Frank Bellamy had come out of his store, as had a few customers, and a scattering of islanders could be seen climbing as fast as they physically could up the hill to the Grange. But there was no sign of the fisherman amongst them.

'Donald! Donald!' she cried, the wind whipping her words away. Then faintly she heard the sound of a diesel engine coughing itself to life. John Dart was already out at sea in the family-owned vessel, Brunhild, but there was a familiar figure in the cabin of the Daisy-Jane. It was Donald.

Racing down the cinder path in her flip-flops, China nearly lost her-footing more than once. But she was too late; the Daisy-Jane was pulling away from the stone jetty into a choppy sea, her blunt nose pointing towards the island of Benbecula. He must have been heading towards Balivanich village where James's company headquarters lay.

'Donald . . . ' she whispered hopelessly towards the storm-tossed boat, as the skies around Butterfly Island began to take on a darker hue. There was only one thing she could do to stop this, no matter what the consequences were between her and her love. She had to warn James McKriven.

* * *

They brought not-so-Handy Andy down on an old shed door torn from one of the Grange's derelict outbuildings. Irene reckoned the break was pretty clean, but the wire-haired handyman was milking the situation for all it was worth. As they took him into The Cuckoo, he was muttering about industrial injury and massive compensation, just as the rain began to fall in large, freezing drops.

'You can cut that out for starters,' Mrs Baxter snapped, holding a medicinal whisky just out of the little man's reach. 'You know China will see you right. Should have landed on your fool head and then you'd have been fine!' Finally, she relinquished her grip on the drink, just as Andy's wife appeared, wailing like a banshee. Whereas he was small and wiry, she was a Valkyrie of a woman. Some years younger than her husband, she had long flaxen hair braided in a ponytail and a fine athletic figure.

'She's Mrs Andy?' China couldn't help herself.

'Either you've got it, or you haven't,' said the little man, being smothered in his wife's bosom, then he gave China his usual saucy wink which told everyone he was on the mend.

'Biddy, a word,' China whispered,

tugging at the landlady's sleeve. 'Donald's stormed off to sort James out.'

'Not before time,' Mrs Baxter sniffed, not being very helpful.

'That's as may be, but the stupid great fool will get himself arrested. We've got to ring ahead and tell someone. You know his temper when it's on the boil. He might even kill McKriven before anyone can stop him!'

The landlady paled slightly at that thought. 'You're right, love. I know the police sergeant in Balivanich. I'll get him to meet Donald when he docks and nip things in the bud.'

China let out a great shuddering sigh of relief. At least it wasn't her who had to do the deed. She was sitting at the bar amidst her notes and her silent laptop when the third island boat, the Jolly Roger, with the doctor on board, docked. That had been another one of her pie-in-the-sky plans, a regular boat service from the main islands to West Uist, financed by charging non-islanders a small fee as any other ferry would, rather than using whoever was free whenever they felt like it. Another part of her marvellous dream. What had she been thinking of, coming up here from the city and playing with everyone's lives as if it were some simple advertising campaign? She was just a simple PA, not some high-flyer executive. The tears of frustration and guilt flowed freely, as she wiped her eyes with the back of her hand. It was all just too hard. Keeping Donald in check was just too hard. Morgan, faithful to the end nuzzled her hand in sympathy, his lead held in his mouth.

'Good idea, boy,' she sniffed, trying to stop feeling sorry for herself. 'Let's get some fresh air.' Grabbing her coat she slipped away unnoticed out of the pub with her canine friend, down the cinder track and onto the path leading back up the hill towards the Grange. Pulling on her new sou'wester hat recently purchased at Bellamy's, she let Morgan tow her up the path amongst the swaying heather and grasses.

Even though she had prepared

herself, the collapsed scaffolding made her gasp when she first saw it. It was a twisted wreck and the lads had been lucky to get away with a few cuts and bruises and Andy's broken leg. She looked up at the stoic grey building, work on the slate roof all but finished. What did she know about property development? And this foolish dream of turning the Grange into a hotel for island visitors that she hadn't even told anyone, was just that — a dream. Having defended Stuart land and property from change all her life, Aunt Bea must be turning in her grave.

The back door was open, so China ducked inside, striding over a piece of scaffolding to do so, anything to get out of the rain. Morgan, impervious to the weather was away foraging in the bushes, so she was completely alone with her self-doubts and misplaced guilt as she wandered back through the ancient house. The money it would have cost to return the place to even being habitable, never mind furniture, en suite bedrooms and so on! She was just a stupid little girl thinking she could change the world and build herself a fairytale life out here in the middle of the sea.

She glanced at her freezing cold feet, wet through and covered in mud. She was still wearing her flip-flops, thanks to her hasty exit from the Inn. She laughed at that, wiggling her muddy toes. 'Can't even wear the right footwear. You're not popping out to the shops for a pint of milk now!'

Sitting down at the foot of the staircase, she tried to curl up in a little ball and disappear. Had it been such a crime to have a dream?

Then a scrap of colour caught her eye. A fluttering of wings. Out of the darkness of the old building came a single butterfly, heading straight for her. Whether it was the same one she'd seen when she had first looked around the Grange what felt like a million years ago, she couldn't be sure, but it was a Red Admiral, all the same, and it settled on the stair banister next to her.

'So, Mrs Butterfly, what do you think I should do? Leave these poor people to live their own lives without my flashy, impossible ideas stirring everything up? Forget trying to tame the mad fisherman?'

The Red Admiral twitched its wings and tiptoed further up the banister. Then a second butterfly fluttered past her nose end, making her start. This one was a Large Heather. It settled on her right coat sleeve. The third winged sliver of colour emerging from the darkness was a Peacock, followed by two more Red Admirals. Soon, there were over thirty of the insects attracted by her body warmth, scattered around her like living confetti. They gave her hope and renewed strength.

First on her new list was sort that man of hers out, if he still wanted her, then she'd see about changing the world. Exhausted, as the butterflies moved about her, she let her head drop into her folded arms and closed her eyes, just for a second. Things would be better if she could just rest for a moment or two. The butterflies would help her sort out her aching head. Just . . . for . . . a . . .

★   ★   ★

The day was bright, the wind warm on her back as China Stuart, aged six years and two months, stood on the stone jetty, shading her eyes with one freckled hand. Against the sun stood the figure of her mother, looking taller than in real life. Worrying about getting all of their luggage on board the pitching fishing boat tied up to the stone jetty.

'Why are we taking so much stuff, Mammy? It's only for a couple of weeks, isn't it?' She had an island accent back then, born on a stormy night with the wind lashing at the window panes, it had given the little girl a sense of fearlessness. She loved the storms that rolled in across the forbidding sea. Ran with the wind and

161

danced in the rain.

'You never know what the weather's going to be like, my darling,' her mother lied. Her eyes, blue like her daughter's, were shadowed in pain. Hiding a fear that only she knew about. A second woman stood on the pier that day. Wrapped all in black, her hair already prematurely white, Aunt Beatrice had come to see them off on their adventure, so why were there tears in her eyes?

'Don't worry auntie, we'll be back before you know it,' the little girl said.

'Aw, my pet, my treasure.' Aunt Bea kissed her again. Her hands were trembling . . . was she ill? 'Are you sure about this, Eve? There are medicines you can take . . . I'm sure if you have another visit from Doctor — '

'Medicine's are no good, Beatrice! China's dad was right. I can't live out here any more. Maybe after a month or two with my feet on dry land . . . ' She left the statement open, passing another case to a silent fisherman.

Down the stone jetty came a tousle-haired boy in a hooped jumper over his shirt and pants that ended just above the knee. He looked about eight years old, with a mucky face and scabs on each leg from countless tumbles down the hillside. His name was Donald Dart and he looked close to tears.

'You sure you're coming back?' he asked the little girl for the tenth time that morning.

'Of course we are, silly. Aren't we, Mammy?' Eve Stuart looked away.

Shyly, Donald bent forward and kissed China clumsily on the cheek. She grimaced and wiped her face with her sleeve. Then the blushing boy whispered something in China's ear. She broke out in a dazzling smile, her eyes alive with delight.

Out of the glare of the sun, the fisherman scooped her up before she could reply to the boy's heartfelt question.

'Come on, wee girl. It's high tide and

we'd better be away. Don't want to leave you behind, do we?' said the fisherman.

The boat suddenly lurched beneath her feet and they were moving, but China hadn't answered her friend's question. He ran alongside them until there was no more jetty left to run on. China waved and waved until her arms were sore as she shouted across the widening gap between the two of them and the sea began to toss the small boat this way and that. But the wind carried her answer to Donald Dart's question away into time . . . nearly thirty years into the future, when China awoke with a start at the foot of the stairs in the abandoned Grange. Around her, the butterflies had gone as mysteriously as they had appeared.

'I remember . . . ' she sighed, her eyes alive with the unwavering spirit of a six year old. 'I remember what Donald asked me on our final day!'

Then she was out of the house and away down the hill as if the devil himself was snapping at her heels.

Morgan appeared from the under-growth and chased after her, barking fit to burst. She remembered, after all his time alone, she remembered. Now all she had to do was find Donald and give him the answer he had been waiting for so long to hear.

9

The stern faced fisherman waved one finger in China Stuart's face. 'You keep away from me! I knew where I was all these years without you! Since you've come back, the whole island's gone mad!'

'Donald!' chided Mrs Baxter, holding China tight as her nephew ranted and raged. 'She's done nothing but try to help! You're the bloody fool who hit a policeman when you docked at Balivanich!'

'Well who told them I'd be coming, eh? I just wanted to get my hands around McKriven's throat but the police were waiting to ambush me!'

'Stop exaggerating, you stupid boy! Sergeant Fitzgerald is sixty if he's a day, and the only other officer on the island is PC Magelan, and she's only twenty years of age! That damn temper of yours, just like your mother, Saints preserve her. You're lucky to get off with a caution! And besides, it was me who rang the police.'

Feeling hurt and betrayed, the fisherman chewed that one over for a second. 'You're just protecting her, like you used to when we were kids. Always took her side when something went missing or got broke, thanks to her clumsy ways! I've had it with the whole lot of you! I'm up to the Grange and tie those sheets back down before this storm starts!' Saying that he barged his way out of the pub and was gone into the driving rain outside.

Biddy Baxter shook her head in despair at her nephew's terrible temper and let China go. 'Better lock all the windows and get out the pots and pans for when the ceiling starts to leak. This storm is going to be a bad one.'

'Will he be alright up the hill on his own?'

'Donald? Let him stew. He owes us both an apology, stupid man!'

Even though it was raining now, the whole island seemed to be cowering in silence as the full might of the storm moved towards them. Lightning played across the sea, its thunder still taking seven or eight seconds to reach West Uist. But then it was six . . . and then it was five.

Doors were being bolted, livestock taken inside and even the massive Irish wolfhound had found himself shelter under one of the pub benches in the snug. Having secured the pub as best they could, Mrs Baxter placed a bottle of whisky on the bar between them and two clean glasses.

'Best way to ride out a storm. May the good Lord protect the men of the sea,' she crossed herself reverently and took her first sip of drink.

China shuddered as the howl of the wind rose an octave, the Inn sign banging against the side of the building and the chairs and benches outside beginning to move in the gale.

'Damn. Should have brought those

in,' fretted the landlady. 'Last time we had weather like this, they ended up across the way and in the sea!'

This was a side of Butterfly Island that China couldn't remember. She was suddenly reminded that it existed in the middle of a cruel ocean; just a chunk of rock jutting up from the sea floor.

'Do you go to the Kirk as often as Aunt Bea?' she asked Mrs Baxter, wanting to talk about anything rather than sit in silence and listen to the storm rage, worrying where her man was.

'Me? If I did, who would run this place? No, your aunt was a force of one. She probably went down to that stone church nearly every day of her life, and that's a lot of days. Well, I told you didn't I, that she even managed to get Donald to harness up the pony and buggy and take her down the day before she died? It was as if she was driven by something. Having to make her peace with God one last time.'

An odd idea began to seep into

China's brain. 'Then that was after you witnessed her write that missing will?'

'The very next day. As I said — driven.'

A shiver ran through China Stuart as an idea burst into a full revelation.

'Oh, Biddy, I think I know where she hid the will! It's been staring us in the face all this time!' Before the landlady could stop her, China was up and pulling on her waterproofs and wellington boots.

'What in heavens name . . . ? Leave the benches outside, love! They were due to be replaced anyway.'

'No, it's the will! Beatrice hid it in the Kirk and I know exactly where!' Unbolting the front door, she was immediately drenched by the storm, but before Mrs Baxter could get round the bar to stop her, she was gone.

'For heaven's sake! Morgan! Go with her you great useless lump!'

The dog looked at the banging front door and the driving rain and then back to the landlady again. Putting his head on his front paws, he shuffled a little further back beneath the pub seat.

* ★ *

All landmarks that China had been getting used to on the narrow paths that laced the island had been rendered invisible as she struggled out into the storm. Immediately something large flew passed her and she instinctively ducked. It was one of the pub benches bowling across the fields as if it were made of balsa wood.

She knew she had to get beyond the jetty, then cut right along a path across the island that led to the cliffs above which the Kirk was suspended, but she was afraid she'd miss the turning. Past the cottages, all shuttered tightly and in darkness, past the general store with the rain pouring down that bright red door . . . it was at that point China thought she should turn back. Wait until the storm was over. But there was a stubborn streak inside her that kept her putting one foot in front of the other. Just a bit further, with the stone jetty now behind her. Just around the next corner. Then she was miraculously out of the worse of the wind, as the shortcut to the Kirk was cut between two high banks of earth.

This was definitely the right path and she only had the torrential rain to fight now. Yet even that blinded her. It forced its way under her hood, beneath her sou'wester and down the back of her neck. She could feel her underwear glued to her as the cold rain soaked her to the skin. Each step became harder to take as she began to shiver with the cold. Whose stupid idea was this? But still she moved forward. One more step . . .

It had come to her in a flash. All that time Aunt Bea spent in prayer whilst Donald shuffled his feet outside the Kirk and waited for her to call him. The perfect time to get a bit of peace and quite, away from everyone mithering her, asking her how she was that day, was she hungry, was she thirsty, how were the aches and pains? Alone in the Kirk she would have had plenty of time to hide a single sheet of paper to make sure that greedy swine James McKriven would never find the will.

The trouble was, neither could anyone else.

There was that twisted tree like an old scarecrow, leaning against the wind. Mangled and bent by years of storms like this. Not far now. Around her the wind eddied and swirled, almost lifting her off her feet. She had to cling to handfuls of grass as she stumbled blindly forward.

Finally, just as she thought she'd gone wrong somewhere along the trail, a shape loomed out of the storm. A simple shaped building from a simpler time. It was the high, ridged roof of the Kirk with its stone cross above the door, and before it were laid out the tombstones amongst which Aunt Bea had been lain to rest. It was at that moment that China's strength nearly gave out. There was a mightly roar from the wind rising up from the cliff behind the stone church, like a living beast. Even one hundred feet above sea level, she could taste the salty spray mixed with the rain in her mouth. Using the grave markers to steady herself, she moved closer to the door. Then, running the last few yards, she was inside the Kirk.

It should have been quieter in there. The roof, regularly repaired better than most of the island's buildings, was strong. But one of the Norman slit windows had blown in and the air was full of pieces of paper, which China realised to her horror were pages from hymnbooks and bibles. Above, as the air pressure built within the building, the roof was beginning to rattle and lift more than it should. She could see the ancient black timbers moving.

Just as she began to move forward, she was thrown off her feet as the door slammed open again behind her. Struggling against the force of the wind, a yellow waterproof suited figure managed to finally get it closed and drop the large rusted latch into place.

It was Donald, thought China, her spirits soaring; he's come to save me! But as the figure turned and lowered his hood, ripping off his dripping wet hat, the hair was black not blonde, the face sarcastic, calculating and unkind. James McKriven stood there, out of breath, his face triumphant.

'I never left the island last night,' he panted, leering at her. 'I knew that sharp little mind of yours would figure out where the old lady had hidden her will. I hid in the empty cottage next to the Inn and watched you. Even in this bloody storm, I knew — ' He was cut off by the cracking of old wood. Above their heads, one of the vast roof beams was beginning to splinter and split.

James glanced down the length of the small church, to the front row pews, to where that tiny family bible sat, still in its place, as if waiting for Beatrice to return and open its pages one last time.

'The crafty old crow hid the will in her bible, didn't she? We all stood right next to it and we didn't know. Just like a Stuart!' Then he made a lunge for the aisle, pushing China to one side. She shouted something at him, but the pistol shots of wood breaking drowned her out. A low rumble and a vibration beneath their feet as the earth turned over in its sleep.

The cliff behind the frail stone building was beginning to fall into the sea.

James McKriven skidded to a halt as the whole Kirk seemed to shift, the floor dropping a good foot at the altar end. Frozen, the two enemies looked up in terror to see the roof peeling away as if it were made of paper, and as the storm dived in, it ripped and tore at anything that wasn't nailed down, the entire alter wall suddenly falling backwards and disappearing. Down the slope the Kirk now sat on, all they could both see was the roaring sea below them, beckoning them on.

Terrified, the will forgotten, James tried to scrabble up the slope towards the distant locked front door, but it was China who stood up and moved forward down the isle of pews. Calmly, the rain pouring down on her from the black sky, she reached forward and picked up her aunt's bible. There was no time to check her theory as she stuffed the book into one deep pocket. Stones were continuing to drop away into the sea as the rest of the Kirk prepared to follow the altar into oblivion.

When she turned to climb back up the slope, James had already opened the door. She was sure he had a clever epitaph for their battles running through his head, but all he mouthed at her through the maelstrom was, 'Goodbye,' before he slammed the door shut in her face.

★ ★ ★

Taking his bad temper out on the twisted scaffolding and the waterproof sheets, Donald had been true to his word and covered the few weak spots left in the Grange roof as best he could. Sheltered by the swaying trees, the wind lost some of its power up here. Nervously he looked at the four tall brick chimney stacks and hoped they would survive this frightening storm.

Then he thought of the spiteful things he had said to his aunt and China, and he felt ashamed. What a fool he was, driving away the one woman he had ever loved, whom he had waited for all these years. Locking up the old house, he pulled his waterproofs tight and began to head back down the hill.

The rain flattened him to the ground as he skidded and slipped in the mud, losing his footing. What had once been hard earth paths were now streams and rivulets of rushing water, so he had to take a different way down, as whole rocks and broken branches were swept down the hillside. He was nearly at the level of the school when a familiar grey shape loomed out of the driving rain:

Morgan, water pouring off him in silver threads flattened the fisherman to the sodden grass with two paws firmly on Donald's chest.

'What are you doing out in the storm, you mad bugger?' he yelled at the hound. Morgan just barked, moving a few feet away and then running back. The dog was a notorious coward when it came to storms. Something urgent must have upset him . . . Then Donald knew; by some sixth sense, he just knew. 'China! What the hell have you done now?' So with one hand gripping tight to Morgan's sodden fur, the fisherman allowed the dog to guide him past the cottages by the pier and down towards the short cut to the Kirk. Man and dog moving as one through the elements, dreading what they were going to find.

The Kirk gave another shudder as more stones peeled away and fell into the wild sea, and China hung on to one of the pews for dear life. If she could just get to the door, she felt sure she could kick it open. Then she made the mistake of looking back to her aunt's pew, now only feet from the new edge of the cliff. There was something sticking out from the shelf below where the family bible had sat. First one, then a second and finally a third spine of the familiar green books could be seen, hidden in the dark cubbyhole.

'Oh, Aunt Bea! You brought those missing journals here to read in peace then forgot them. All the family secrets — you wrote about them in those books!' She stopped half way to safety. Watching the pew as it shivered and moved a closer to the abyss. She had to go back for the journals. As she turned again to inch her way down the slope, the door creaked open once again. In its stone archway was another figure, but this time she recognized the grey eyes and the light coloured hair.

'Donald! Aunt Bea's journals — all the answers — they're in her pew!'

He could see what China was about to do. 'Reach out and take my hand!'

He shouted above the wind. 'Let them go! I can't lose you again!'

'But . . . ' she began, as Donald lunged towards her and grasped her arm.

'Come back,' he whispered in her ear. 'Come home.'

So she closed her eyes and buried her face into his chest as he guided the pair of them to safety. It was only when they got to the Kirk door that she could see a second figure lying prone amongst the gravestones.

'I met James coming out, so I knew you'd be here,' he grinned, rubbing the bruised knuckles on his right hand.

There was another shiver beneath their feet, as more of the stone church dropped into the sea. Even though she had hopefully found the will, China closed her eyes again and fought back the tears at the thought of all those written memories gone for ever. Then she opened them in surprise as Donald shouted, 'You mad dog! What on earth?'

Hopping over the doorstep, Morgan dropped three familiar books at China's feet. As they had struggled to get out of the collapsing church, for some reason the dog had got it into his head to retrieve Beatrice's diaries, seconds before the Stuart pew slipped into the sea.

'Good dog!' China and Donald said in unison, China quickly picking the books up from the grass and spiriting them away inside her coat before they got too wet. Morgan, unused to that particular phrase being directed at him, cocked his head to one side and looked puzzled. In the howling storm, with parts of the cliff still sliding away into oblivion, the lovers somehow found themselves laughing at the trusty hound.

10

After all the high adventures, it was typical of China to catch a streaming cold. Dressed in her Hello Kitty PJs, she could be found wandering around the pub quoting lines about her childhood from the rescued journals, to anyone who would listen. Those books and a man-sized box of tissues were her constant companions for the better part of a week. Then, or course, there was Morgan — keeping an eye on his new charge.

Somehow between them, Donald and China had dragged the unconscious body of James McKriven back down the twisting paths and to the safety of the Inn, with Morgan bravely leading the way. As James came around, a captive of all the people he had tried so hard to ruin, they found his sidekick, Japes hiding in the empty cottage next door and locked the pair of them in the pub cellar.

Exhausted and dripping wet, China lay the small Stuart bible on the bar counter as her friends gathered round. Like a magician, she opened the book at where a black ribbon marked a page, and there it was — a single sheet of paper written on one side in her aunt's familiar hand, witnessed by Mrs Baxter. She had found the last will.

The next day, the sea was as calm as a duck pond and the islanders came out of their homes to assess the damage. The first boat in was the police from Benbecula to pick up James and his henchman, who had been babbling non-stop all night about the crimes they had committed. Where as James McKriven was charged with attempted murder, after China described how he had tried to lock her in the doomed Kirk, Martin Japes was charged with tampering with scaffolding up at the Grange. Everyone gathered in silence to watch the two handcuffed men being lead in shame onto the boat. There were no last bitter words from James McKriven, he knew when he was beaten.

'Sergeant Fitzgerald's been dying to try out those cuffs for years,' Mrs Baxter remarked casually, causing a nervous round of laughter to move through the crowd.

★　★　★

Despite her streaming cold, which kept China and Donald at arms' length for a few days, she managed to move all the plans forward for the island's rescue. 'National Heritage is already inspecting what's left of the Kirk. They say it's quite feasible to move the remains and by rescuing most of the original stones from the base of the cliff, they can rebuild it further inland. With the Lottery grant I've applied for, we should be able to construct a concrete wall on the shore to prevent any more cliff erosion.

'We've the Press heading in to report the storm and the damage to the 14th century Kirk — evidently it's the only one of its kind still partially standing. All that publicity can only help attract more businesses to the island. The phone company are already going to pay a disgusting amount of money for a new satellite mast around the other side of the hill on Stuart land. What we get from that will rebuild both boatsheds and then some!'

The list went on and on. Now it had been proved that China was the legal beneficiary of all her aunt's property, things could really get moving. But it was the quiet moments during all the comings and goings that China enjoyed the best. Wrapped up in bed, with Morgan squeezed in down the side of her like a great hot water bottle — all be it a slightly smelly one — reading her aunt's journals and finding all the missing pieces of her life. Then there were the meals for two by candlelight in one corner of the snug, as she dressed in her best and her and Donald got to know each other by just talking and talking.

Finally, looking fit and well again, she gathered the group of friends for a celebratory drink and the official launch of the Butterfly Island Sanctuary.

'Reading Aunt Bea's diaries, I've finally managed to find out why my mother and I left the island,' she announced when there was a lull in the business conversation. 'All the tales of Mum and Dad fighting, Aunt Bea throwing Mum out, great family rows up at the Grange, all have a grain of truth in them. This is what really happened.'

Life on Butterfly Island had all started to go wrong for the Stuarts when Eve Stuart was diagnosed as having agoraphobia. It wasn't just the fear of wide open spaces, but the fear of panic attacks brought on by the insecurity of where she was. Living on a tiny dot of rock in the middle of a wide open sea and beneath the endless skies became the worse place for Eve to be. China's father, Campbell, had wanted them to leave the island and find a more secure home on the mainland, where his wife could receive proper medical attention. That was what started the rows, as Eve refused, saying her husband's duties to the island, his Aunt and the Stuart line had to come first. That she would 'muddle through'.

But the panic attacks grew more frequent and more violent. It was as Campbell started to make arrangements for them to leave Butterfly Island, that the tragic accident at sea happened, where he was washed overboard from the Brunhild and never seen again. Eve had lost her love and her best friend; the only person who could talk the fears away. She now spent the entire time locked away in a single room in the Grange with little China, so Bea and Eve made the sad decision together; China and her mother had to leave the island.

'Aunt Bea was devastated. They kept

in touch for some years, but normal stuff like paying bills, shopping, or writing a letter just became too hard for Mum. We were drifting about so much as she found casual night-time cleaning jobs, that they lost contact with each other,' explained China to her captive audience. 'Why Mum never told me all this stuff, I'll never know. I guess she thought there was always tomorrow, she'd tell me the next day. Then she died suddenly of heart problems, the past was lost and I created a new life for myself. I wish I could tell her how sorry I was for all the things I thought about her, all the things I said, but I can't. So now I'm here to stay, if you'll have me, and I can finally lay the past to rest.'

★   ★   ★

The sky was that shade of china blue Eve Stuart had named her daughter after, and the sea like a mirror, as Donald and his love stood hand in hand above the fields that led down from the Grange. It was that time of year once again. That moment the two of them had always spent together when the butterflies hatched.

'The old temper is holding out well, Donald,' she sighed, glad for a perfect moment together like this.

'I like your way of shutting me up when I go off on one. Silenced with a kiss. But I think I let off a head of steam by punching McKriven out in the storm. You should have seen it — bop! Down he went!'

'Well you make sure you don't build up that head of steam again, mister, or you're chucked!' She laughed to defuse his discomfort and snuggled close. 'I remembered, by the way.'

'Remembered what?'

'The words you whispered to me the day we left. 'China Stuart — when we're grown will ye marry me?' you said.'

'And?'

'Oh, go on then. That cottage next to the Inn is going begging. We'll have to lock Morgan in the kitchen at nights though, he'll get jealous.'

'He'll howl.' Morgan's head went to one side as he heard his name mentioned. 'Bad dog — whoa, here we go!'

Below them, as the sun rose to its height and warmed the rock strewn fields, the first few scarps of colour began to flutter up from the long grass. Holding each other's hands tight, as they had so long ago, the two lovers ran laughing down the hillside and a vast cloud of butterflies of every colour rose up before them and fluttered away into the endless sky, their dog bouncing along with them barking all the way.

It was then that China Stuart knew that she had finally come home.

THE END

We do hope that you have enjoyed reading this large print book.

Did you know that all of our titles are available for purchase?

We publish a wide range of high quality large print books including:
Romances, Mysteries, Classics
General Fiction
Non Fiction and Westerns

Special interest titles available in large print are:
The Little Oxford Dictionary
Music Book, Song Book
Hymn Book, Service Book

Also available from us courtesy of Oxford University Press:
Young Readers' Dictionary
(large print edition)
Young Readers' Thesaurus
(large print edition)

For further information or a free brochure, please contact us at:
Ulverscroft Large Print Books Ltd.,
The Green, Bradgate Road, Anstey,
Leicester, LE7 7FU, England.
Tel: (00 44) 0116 236 4325
Fax: (00 44) 0116 234 0205